ROUSSAN
PUBLISHERS INC.
Specializing in YA and fiction for pre-teens

THE CANADA COUNCIL | LE CONSEIL DES ARTS
FOR THE ARTS | DU CANADA
SINCE 1957 | DEPUIS 1957

We acknowledge the support of the Canada
Council for the Arts for our publishing program.

We acknowledge the financial support of the Government
of Canada through the Book Publishing Industry
Development Program (BPIDP) for our publishing activities.

The author wishes to thank to the Canada Council of the Arts for their financial
assistance in the completion of this book.

http://www.roussan.com

Copyright ©2000 by Lillian Boraks-Nemetz

National Library of Canada
Bibliothèque nationale du Québec

Canadian Cataloguing in Publication Data

**Boraks-Nemetz, Lillian, 1933-
The Lenski file**

(On time's wing)

ISBN 1-896184-76-6

I. Title. II. Series.

PS8553.O732L45 2000   jC813'.54 C00-900829-2   PZ7.B64765Le 2000
PZ7.B64765Su 1999

Cover design by Dan Clark
Cover art by Carol Biberstein
Interior design by Jean Shepherd

Typeface Sabon 10.9

Published simultaneously in Canada and the United States of America
Printed in Canada

1 2 3 4 5 6 7 8 9 UTP 8 7 6 5 4 3 2 1 0

In memory of my grandmother who saved my life
and my sister whom I shall always seek.

Contents

The Lenski File

I am packing!

The old brown suitcase lies on my bed like an empty boat waiting for cargo. The bed is a sea of objects, drifting from one spot to another, never finding their rightful resting place. I am a tide flooding the bed with junk.

What's the use? I can't take all this stuff anyway. I pick out the necessities and begin to fill the suitcase: lingerie, shoes, a skirt, a pair of pants, a dress, three blouses. A volume of French Canadian poetry in English translation. Several novels. A folder of my latest translations of Polish poetry. I must put in a writing pad as well. Have to be professional about this. I search my cluttered desk with impatient hands and finally find the pad attached to a red folder of notes. I almost forgot.

The mysterious file.

I found it yesterday while snooping around my step-father Max's desk looking for stamps. As always, my curiosity settled on the one drawer Max keeps locked at all times. To my absolute shock, this time the key was in the hole. Without hesitation, I turned the key. The drawer slid out easily toward me.

Files. How boring.

Absent-mindedly, I thumbed through the beige folders, in alphabetical order. A red folder stood out from the rest. It was filed under the letter *L*. I lifted it out. The words "Lenski File" were neatly written on the label.

I knew nothing about the existence of a "Lenski File," but decided that it must have belonged to Papa rather than my stepfather, whose name is Steiner.

Clutching it in my hands like a precious object, I took the file into the kitchen, poured myself a glass of chocolate milk, and started to browse. I was astounded.

The documents were from 1945. The paper was already beginning to yellow and there was dust among the pages. As I flipped through them, each felt as fragile as a leaf on a winter tree, save for the first three pages.

These were heavy with pasted-on black and white photographs I had never before seen:

The First Image
Myself, in the country, on my grandfather's estate, the
Rose Villa in the village of Malinow, in Poland. I am
riding a tricycle along a path between two flower
beds. I am wearing a striped sweater. My curly blond
hair is tied up with a big white bow. I am happy,
laughing, like a child at a puppet show.

The Second Image

Two heads together: Babushka's close to mine, hers large, mine small, topped by a crown of plaited hair with a white flower on the side. We look happy together in spite of the war and hiding away from the Nazis.

The Third Image

An older gentleman—semi-bald, tall, elegant, in a dark suit. He is walking down a peaceful Warsaw street. My grandfather, Samuel Bernard Lenski, murdered by a Nazi officer in the Warsaw ghetto in front of his apartment, before his horrified son, my father.

The Fourth Image

An angelic little girl with blond curls and a pug nose is seated in the grass with two small children, a boy on one side and a girl on the other. She is wearing a dress with flowers on it. My little sister, Basia, who disappeared somewhere in Poland. It's summer. Even in a black and white photo one can see this calm country background lit up by the sun shining on the grass, the bushes and the trees. But it's 1943, and my sister is hiding from the Nazis.

The Fifth Image

Two young men in a field leaning against a huge pile of hay. Relaxed and smiling in the hot summer sun of the Polish countryside, looking comfortable with each other, as only two close friends can look. Papa and his childhood friend, Roman Mortynski. He and his wife took in my sister Basia as their adopted Christian child to protect her from the Nazis.

Five photographs of faces frozen in time. Faces I've tried so hard to remember.

As for those documents! I was amazed at their existence and at the same time terribly curious. I didn't think we had any documents at all. I often regretted not having spoken with my father about our family history or the genocide. There was so much to know, questions about Basia, our properties in Poland. Mother and I never discussed the past. All I had were my own memories. Why hadn't I been told about this? Why didn't my parents consider that I, too, experienced all kinds of feelings and had memories?

Mother was very secretive about those days. Maybe it hurt too much to talk about it, and maybe she had forgotten all about these photos. I wished she would at least validate my life during the war. I needed to talk about it. Instead, it had been locked up in a drawer as if nothing had ever happened to any of us.

Just as I was about to survey a court document written in Polish legal jargon, Mama came into my room to give me some tips on travelling. Then Max walked in offering me pocket money and his cousin Lola's address in London where he thought I should stay, rather than at my friend Dorothea's.

When I finally settled down again to read the documents, my five-year-old sister, Pyza, marched in with all her dolls, whose hair had to be done before I left. There was no time that evening to read the file.

Now, in the midst of the chaos in my room, I give up

packing and once again try to concentrate on these pages, some typed, some handwritten in Polish.

The front door slams. I hear voices in the hall. Mama, Max, and Pyza are back from shopping. Annoyed, I hide the file again under some clothing and books. I'll never get to read these documents.

What now?

Max pokes his head in. "I've got your passport here, and your itinerary." How nice. When he realized that I was going to go to England in spite of his veto, he decided to be helpful.

"Thanks, Max," I say warmly, and I mean it, though my heart and mind are still on that red file.

Adam is coming over tonight to say goodbye, and I've got to finish this packing! Resigned, I slide the file to the bottom of my suitcase. I'll read it while I'm away, then when I return I'll sneak it back into Max's other drawer, the one he doesn't lock, and I'll hide it underneath all his letters. When he finds it, he'll think he misplaced it. Besides, I can't worry about it now, there is still so much left to do.

I lock the suitcase and stand it up against the wall.

"Slava!" Mama calls out. "Adam is here!"

Rats! I am not looking forward to this. Adam refuses to understand why I am going to England, and the last time I'd seen him, we'd argued about it. He doesn't approve of my going away any more than Mama and Max do. They are all just "putting up with it."

Adam is sitting in the living room, his feet up on the coffee table. Mama hates this, but forgives him because he comes from a very good Vancouver family. She thinks that when I marry him, I'll be able to teach him good manners. They really want me to marry Adam, because there is hardly any room for me in this apartment and I don't have a job. If I didn't babysit Pyza, I'd be considered useless.

"Hi Ad!" I say, trying my best to sound friendly.

"Hullo, Liz," says Adam flatly, calling me by my Canadian name.

"How's studying?" I ask. Adam studies hard, and is taking extra summer courses to complete Law School.

"Oh, not bad," he answers matter-of-factly. "Lots of work." There is a long, uncomfortable silence between us.

"But there is something I need to say to you," he begins awkwardly, twirling a pencil, which he always wears behind his ear. "I still don't understand what you're doing. Who are these poets you're so driven to? How can you," he is becoming angry now, "suddenly decide to leave everything and go away, just like that?"

This is a repeat of our last conversation. He'd seemed pleased when I told him that I had won a prize for my poetry translations. But when I added that I had been invited to England to give a reading of the poems, Adam had exploded.

Mama and Max had also put me through an interrogation. They absolutely refused to let me go! But for once I stood up for myself and rebelled against their decision, and, finally, they reluctantly acquiesced. After all, I was no longer a child. I was almost nineteen years old.

I felt manipulated by all three of them. Would there always be somebody other than me deciding my fate? I had thought that my days of guilt-ridden feelings were over. Why shouldn't I feel free to do as I please, providing it didn't hurt anyone else?

I find my voice with difficulty.

"Adam, I love writing and translating. I love poetry and prose, and I love books. I don't enjoy playing cards, or discussing banalities with our friends, like gossip, or where to go for a hamburger!" I find it hard to catch my breath. "You shouldn't stop me from doing what I like. I wouldn't stop you from practising law."

"That's different," replies Adam, pouting like Max. They both have a petulant bottom lip. "Law is my future."

He hasn't really heard a word I said. He has one standard for himself and another for me. He assumes, like Max, that I couldn't live off my kind of work, and therefore his is more important and more serious.

"Look," I try to philosophize, "if we were meant to be, you and me, then when I return we'll be together again."

"And if you don't? Then what?"

I can't respond to this.

"Liz, I love you and want to marry you someday. You'll have to choose. Me or the rest of the world."

Pressured again! I feel both flattered and disgusted at the same time. Is this some kind of a proposal? I can't possibly choose.

"Papa once said, 'Give a loved one their wings and let them fly away. If they truly love you, they'll return of their own free will, and in their own time'." I sound like a preacher.

"I wish I could believe that," says Adam sarcastically. "This 'loved one' may decide to take five years to return, in which case I wouldn't be willing to wait. I have to go now. Have a great trip.

"By the way," he continues dryly, "how about I join you in Montreal for Miriam's wedding?" He is testing me, watching my expression. Then, attempting a half-smile, he pecks me on the cheek and leaves.

Adam at Miriam's wedding? He wasn't even invited!

He really doesn't understand my feelings, only his own. Maybe I don't understand his either. I return to my room and find Mama sitting on my bed.

"I heard everything," she exclaims proudly.

"That's eavesdropping, Mama."

"So what? You're not my daughter?"

"So don't you have any respect for me, Mama?" I answer in the same tone of voice.

"Do something that I should respect you for. Finish university. You're a dropout!"

"You and Max wouldn't let me take the Arts, only the Sciences so I could have a 'well-paying profession.' I am no good at science. Neither of you wants to give me the education I need. Max just wants me to work in a lousy store, dressing dummies."

"Even there you got fired!"

"Just because I put a dress on a male dummy. That doesn't make me stupid. I simply wasn't paying attention. I didn't deserve to get fired. It was this girl in whom I confided about being a Jewish immigrant. She got me fired."

"I don't know what will become of you, Slava. You should marry someone steadfast like Adam, and be secure, instead of schlepping around the world!"

We sit in silence. Lately this has become our greatest form of communication.

"I have to go now," Mama says. "We're playing bridge at Olga's."

My last night at home and they go out and leave me to babysit, I think resentfully as I watch Mama leave the room in that regal manner of hers.

I pack my few toiletries and some more reading stuff into a carry-on bag. Afterwards, I read Pyza a bedtime story about Cinderella. Maybe I, too, am getting ready to go to a great ball. I just hope I won't turn into a pumpkin.

Life's Strange Alterations

I am finally on my way to London.

The airplane is bouncing up and down. The engines growl in protest. The effect is vertigo and clogged ears.

My bottle of Coke turns over and spills onto the curly head of a two-year-old girl waddling down the aisle.

She begins to cry bitterly.

She looks up at me with big, innocent green eyes that look hurt, while her mouth sucks in the sweetness of the cold Coke dripping down her face. Her father sweeps her up and carries her back into the safety of a seatbelt.

She reminds me of Basia, in that black and white photo I found in the Lenski File. I last saw my sister in Mama's arms, just before she left our shabby room in the Warsaw ghetto. It was 1942. Basia went to a Polish village to stay with some Christian friends. A year later we learned that she might have been murdered by the Gestapo. We were never sure what really happened to her. But I remember how we tried to find her in convents and orphanages right after the war. Searching all those little faces, hoping, praying.

That was 1945.

It's now 1952.

I still hope to find her someday.

The little girl toddles back up the aisle. I offer her a candy. Her plump fingers reach out for it and she toddles back to her seat, calling, "Mama, Mama," waving the candy in mid-air.

The pilot announces a storm over the prairies. The insecurity of hanging in the clouds and the wobbling of the plane bother me. I feel like turning to my neighbour for consolation, but the young man's arms are entwined around a woman sitting on his other side. So I grip the arms of my chair with both hands to steady myself.

How did I get into this weird situation in the first place? I wouldn't be here if it weren't for the two letters sent to me from two very different people.

Out the window, the charcoal-grey mass of cloud provides an excellent lens for daydreaming. I am zooming along the abstract highway of time. As always, in order to move ahead in my life, I need to travel backwards, to see how the past can affect the present and even the future. Life's strange alterations!

The first letter that changed my life was from Miriam, who was my best friend when I lived in Montreal. It also indirectly concerned my very first boyfriend, Joshua.

Miriam wrote:

April 30, 1952

Dearest Polachka,

A short note to let you know of my forthcoming marriage. I met a wonderful man in Israel, Michael Freeman. He is from Montreal, but came to do some research at a hospital in Tel Aviv. We fell in love instantly. I want you to be my maid of honour, Slava. Please don't refuse. I still consider you my dearest friend and I want your blessing.

Joshua and I are great pals. There was never any chemistry between us, even though we did come together in our grief over your absence, and the excitement about going to Israel. I know, though, that somewhere inside, deeply hidden, he still has a love for you. You must come. I'll even send you a ticket. And you can stay with us. The wedding is August the eleventh at the Temple. The colour theme of the wedding is purple and blue. Your dress will be blue, and mine white of course. I'll send you material and a picture of your gown. Save the bill, it's on me. Please write soon.

All my love
Miriam

Should I accept the invitation, I wondered. I couldn't believe that Josh still loved me. Surely he had another girl-friend by now. Besides, how could I suddenly become a loving friend and maid of honour to Miriam?

How could I face Joshua and Miriam as if nothing had happened?

The young man next to me reminds me of him. Joshua

whom I loved, and whom I still love. I have so many pictures of him in my head:

Joshua in his blue sweater at fifteen, offering help with English to a Polish immigrant: me.

Joshua teaching her about being Jewish.

Joshua presenting her with a menorah and lighting the Hanukkah candles.

Joshua, a proud Jew, shielding her from those who tried to discriminate against her.

Joshua encouraging her to write the stories of her childhood, about surviving the Nazi genocide.

Joshua, the best young basketball player in Eastern Canada, and the best student.

Joshua confessing his love for her.

Joshua heartbroken, saying goodbye at the train station as she leaves Montreal to live in Vancouver with Mama, her second sister, Pyza, and stepfather Max.

Joshua sounding unhappy about her not writing to him.

Joshua fed up and turning to her best friend Miriam. The two of them taking off for a kibbutz in Israel, together.

It was partly my fault, I guess. At first I didn't write because I was ashamed. I thought that Josh would hate me if he knew that, at boarding school, I chose not to tell anyone for the longest time that I was Jewish. The war and the suffering had made me doubt God. A doubt that not even Joshua could have removed.

Misinterpreting my silence, and thinking that I had stopped caring, Josh had turned to Miriam.

The truth was, I still loved God, and my two friends, but I couldn't completely forgive them for having hurt me. In an effort to block out the memory of Josh, I turned to Adam, whom I met in Vancouver. As for God, I feel closer to him now than ever before, particularly on this plane.

In answer to Miriam's invitation, one part of my brain said a big "No." Then, in another part, a little bell of longing for Montreal began to ring, and the fat cat of curiosity about my two best friends began to stalk me. How would all this turn out?

After a brief argument, my brain said, "Yes."

The second fateful letter was thick. It was from Tadeusz Skovronek, a thirty-year-old Polish writer I had met in Qualicum Beach last summer, when he was visiting from England.

He wrote in Polish:

May 1, 1952

Dear Slava,

Thank you for the last batch of translations of Andrzej Mur's poems. They were excellent. The editor only had a few corrections to make. Did you hear me? An editor! This means that your translations have been accepted for publication, but we need another twenty-five poems to make a book. Can you do it? Here are more poems just in case. The subsidy for the publication will probably come either from a Polish Foundation of Assistance for Immigrant Artists, or the British Arts Council. Either way you'll get paid something and maybe you'll even be invited to London for a reading with the author of both the Polish and the English versions of his work. I am excited. Are you? By the way, I liked very much your translation of some of my poems, as well.

Please write soon and let me know your decision.

Affectionately

Tad

My fingers fumbled with the folded pages inside the envelope. Poems and more poems by Andrzej Mur! How could I do all that work? Besides, Mother and Max would never let me go as far as London, especially if they knew about Tadeusz, the older man in my life! On the other hand, I argued, how could I miss such an opportunity?

My decision was swift. Even before consulting Mama and Max, I wrote Tad an enthusiastic note saying that if such an invitation became a reality, I'd be happy to come.

By that time, Mama and Max had become somewhat softer about my going to Miriam's wedding. This was the first step.

I also wrote to Dorothea, my friend from the boarding school in Victoria, to take her up on the invitation to stay with her in London. Then I began translating the poems.

I had trouble with some of the Polish expressions, which sounded good only in Polish. After I laboured for days and days, each Polish poem rendered in English seemed a miracle.

Mama wanted to know what I did for hours alone in my room. I wasn't studying, I wasn't working, why were my eyes so tired-looking? I told her I was translating some

Polish poetry. She didn't comment one way or the other.

Toward the middle of May, I had finished all twenty-five poems. I decided to go to the English Department at the University of British Columbia and ask if a student could check my English grammar. Preferably one who studied poetry.

The secretary gave me several names and I picked one. Geoffrey White, a student of Shakespeare, read over the poems. They needed only a few corrections. My translations of metaphors and my English equivalents for certain Polish expressions remained untouched. I did the corrections quickly and sent the work to London, by special delivery.

I waited impatiently for a reply.

It came sooner than I expected. The poems were accepted for publication. Tad enclosed a money order, enough for a ticket to London and some to spare. I arranged for a stopover in Montreal on the way back so I could go to Miriam's wedding.

Going to London became an obsession. I knew about Big Ben, the Waterloo Bridge, Piccadilly Square, and Princess Elizabeth—now Queen Elizabeth—in Buckingham Palace. I knew all this from reading, movies, and Movietone News. Also, England was Europe, and Europe pulled me like a magnet.

We've just left Winnipeg. It'll be hours before we reach London. The stewardess is serving lunch. I admire her grace and composure. The red juice in the tomato salad reminds me of my fateful meeting with Tadeusz

Skovronek at Qualicum Beach.

Last summer, after graduating from high school, Dorothea, my upper-class English friend, and I went to work as waitresses at an inn at Qualicum Beach on Vancouver Island. Dorothea had become my best friend at St. Anne's Boarding School For Girls. When I asked why she would want to take on this kind of work, she told me that her parents were getting a divorce, and she didn't want to go home.

Mama and Max (particularly Max) were delighted at the prospect of my new job. With the money I would earn, I'd be able to enter university in the fall.

Before long I was on the Princess Marguerite ferry, going back to Victoria.

Miss Basil-Stubbs, the headmistress of the school, drove Dorothea and me to the Chez Lion Lodge.

We were like rag dolls by dinnertime on our first day. What did we know about waitressing? The head of the lodge, Vivian, was never there to instruct us. Instead she left us to her bossy niece, Bonnie, who did nothing but laugh at us.

At lunch and dinner Bonnie usually sat at the family's reserved table. I was to serve her. She had an unpleasant manner which I tried to ignore. One day at lunch, when I was waiting on a million people, she called me over.

"Take this note to that gentleman over there. Right now," she commanded, handing me a folded piece of paper.

The gentleman she spoke of was a handsome blonde-haired, blue-eyed young man sitting with another young man at a nearby table.

Feeling embarrassed at being used as a go-between, I went over to them and asked whether they wanted more coffee.

"The young lady sitting over there," I said, pointing with my head to where Bonnie was, "asked me to give you this note." I handed him the note. He took it, following my eyes to where Bonnie was sitting.

As I poured the coffee, I could see over his shoulder what she had written: "If you're not doing anything tonight, come to cabin 11 at nine o'clock."

Disgusting, I thought. Then I gave Bonnie the benefit of the doubt. Maybe they knew each other from before.

The young man scribbled a note. "This is for the young lady, Bonnie," he said, then turned back to his companion. I felt dismissed.

I delivered the note to Bonnie. Then Vivian motioned me into the kitchen. Just as I approached the open door, Dorothea rushed out with two platters of food. There was a loud collision, and I ended up on the floor with tomato sauce and spaghetti mashed into my blouse and skirt. All I could feel was bewilderment and discomfort as the hot mush slithered through my clothing and down my skin.

Then came the feeling of shame. Everyone in the dining room was staring at me. Suddenly, I felt someone's arms lifting me up from the back. I raised my head and saw the young man with the note looking at me with concern.

"Are you all right?" he inquired. Despite my consternation I could detect a foreign accent.

"Yes, I'm fine," I replied weakly. Vivian looked angry. Dorothea was wiping up the mess. Bonnie smirked at me, still sitting at her table.

"You'd better go and change your clothes," said Vivian, in a funereal tone of voice. I was only too happy to disappear. Reeking of tomato and garlic, I ran as fast as I could to the cabin and got out of my gooey clothes, then flopped onto the bed and wept.

After I calmed down, I began to dress. I had barely managed to change my uniform when there was a knock on the door. I went to open it, and there stood the young man who had helped me up.

"I hope I am not intruding. I only followed you here to see if you were all right," he said politely with that same foreign accent. "My name is Tadeusz," he added. "What's yours?"

A charge of excitement ran through me. This young man had a Polish first name.

"I'm fine," I said, replying to his questions in order, "and my name is Elizabeth Slava Lenski."

"What nationality are you?" asked Tadeusz.

"I have just become a Canadian, but I was born in Poland. We came here only five years ago."

"I would like to talk to you. Could you meet me at nine o'clock by the red maple in the garden?"

I felt caught off guard. "I don't know," I mumbled. "What about your date with Bonnie?" I seemed to be stepping deeper and deeper into mud.

Tadeusz grinned. "Don't worry about Bonnie. I've

straightened that out. Where I come from girls wait to be asked out. Besides, I don't like aggressive women. See you later," he said on his way out, sounding sure of himself.

I sort of liked this man and wanted to get to know him better. After a brief soul-search, I decided that I would meet Tadeusz.

Dorothea reminded me that we were not allowed to socialize with the hotel guests, so I'd need to be careful.

At five minutes past nine I was by the maple tree shaking hands with Tadeusz. "Please call me Tad," he said. "It's easier to say in English." I would just as soon have called him by his full Polish name, Tadeusz. I told him about having to change my name from Slava to Elizabeth, in order to sound less foreign. "After that, I became sort of foreign to myself," I said. "Elizabeth still sounds strange to me."

"How about my calling you Slava?" he asked. I told him that would be wonderful. He spoke in Polish and I was absolutely thrilled. There was no one I knew in Vancouver with whom I could speak Polish, except Mama.

Tadeusz told me that he was thirty years old and had left Poland for London, England, several years ago. He lived there now, studying journalism and writing articles for two small Polish newspapers, one in London, one in Warsaw. His main job was to report on the newest writers and their poetry and prose styles. He said that he wrote poetry in Polish, that he was a non-practising Catholic and that his last name was Skovronek.

His last name meant "skylark" in English. How appropriate for a poet.

"Do you publish your poetry?" I asked.

"Only in Polish newspapers and journals. Unfortunately, we immigrants have a small audience. What about you?"

I told him that I wrote poetry and small prose pieces, but that my English was too weak for me to be a good writer, as was my Polish, since I had to abandon it when I came to Canada in 1947.

"Why were you forced to abandon Polish?" he asked.

"Because everyone I met spoke English, and my parents urged me to forget Polish and Poland, and learn to speak English."

Tad looked at me in disbelief. "Abandon your own roots and heritage?" he asked.

I told him about being in Poland during the Nazi persecution of Jews, first in the Warsaw ghetto, then escaping and hiding under a false identity.

He listened with great concentration. I felt oddly liberated after this outpouring. There were so few people I could talk to about these things. Even though Tad was not Jewish, he too had experienced the war as a child.

Tad was silent for a long moment. "I didn't expect any of this from you," he said quietly. "You speak good English and behave like a native."

"I've learned to put on a front. People don't like foreigners."

He nodded in agreement. "It's somewhat different in Europe. But I do understand what happened to Jews during the war, though there is a tendency in Poland to ignore it. There was a Jewish woman living in our attic. My

27

mother always carried trays of food up to her. Once she got sick and I had to do it. I felt sorry for the poor woman, stuck up in the attic for almost four years."

"Weren't your parents afraid of the consequences? To hide a Jew meant instant death."

"My father was against it," replied Tadeusz, "but after he joined the Polish Partisans, he didn't care. He was never home anyhow."

"Did the Jewish woman pay your mother?"

"The woman offered us money, but my mother only took what was necessary for food, even though we were very poor and had hardly anything to eat. She felt it was her duty to help this woman.

"But I know," he added quickly, "that there were Polish folks in our town who made money out of hiding Jews. Of course, there were good folks, too."

So he did know about it.

"What town are you from?" I asked.

"Kolkov."

My heart jumped into my throat. Basia. That's where she had been hiding. Where they said she had been murdered. But I said nothing.

I heard rustling. There was someone else in the garden.

"Good evening," said a voice out of the darkness. It was Bonnie. "Are you two enjoying yourselves?" she said flippantly, now visible in front of the maple tree. "And what's this foreign language I hear?"

"The language is Polish," said Tadeusz, politely but firmly. "If you will excuse us, I was just walking Elizabeth to her cabin."

He took my arm and guided me away, while Bonnie stood speechless under the tree.

"I have to leave the day after tomorrow," said Tadeusz, handing me a few pieces of paper. "Here is my address in London and a poem written by my friend Andrzej Mur. He is a Polish émigré, like you, who now lives in England. And here," Tadeusz pulled a notepad from his breast pocket and tore a page out of it, "is a poem I wrote this morning on Qualicum Beach. Perhaps you could try to translate it into English. If it's good, I'll try to get it published in a literary magazine, then send you the money, if there is any."

I was disappointed that he was leaving so soon, but he explained that he was here to visit his cousin, who was showing him the sights of Vancouver Island.

"I will come tomorrow evening to say goodbye." He put his arms around me and kissed me on both cheeks.

"For a young girl," he remarked, "you express yourself in a very mature way. I guess the war taught you to become an adult awfully fast," he added, then disappeared into the shadows. I marvelled at what he had said. Only one person, a teacher at St. Anne's, had said these things to me before.

I could still smell the mint on his skin. My feet were glued to the ground. The papers he had given me slipped out of my hands, while my arms hung limply. All this was so unexpected. I felt as if some strange fate had brought me to Qualicum Beach.

There was no way I could sleep before reading the poem Tad had given me.

I read it hungrily. It was beautiful and moving.

I picked up a pen and wrote a quick English translation in the exercise book where I had been scribbling my own poems. As I translated I felt a thrill I couldn't understand. From a language few people here understood, I had created a meaningful English poem. I also translated the poem by A. Mur which Tad had included among the papers.

The next day he came to the cabin as promised. I was alone, as Dorothea had gone out to give us some space. It took a while before I got up enough courage to let him read my translation of his poem. It was getting dark and the trees were giant silhouettes against a dark blue sky. The scent of roses, mixed with the smell of dung from a nearby pile of manure, wafted in.

"They're marvellous," he said quietly, having read both translations. "Marvellous. You really are a poet. Only a poet could translate verse so well."

I wanted to jump up and down like a little kid, but checked myself.

"I'll show them to Mur, and if he likes them I'll send you a whole lot to translate."

By now I felt a curious bond with Tad. Once again, when he held me close to him, I could hardly catch my breath. There was something so sweet about him, so appealing. Of course I was no connoisseur of men. Particularly ones who were so much older than I.

After he left I felt sad, but not for long. "Somehow," my intuition whispered, "you'll see him again."

The plane still feels like a whirling carousel. I comfort myself with the thought that the exit door is just one seat away. The pilot announces we are over Montreal.

Montreal. Where Papa died two years ago. Where Miriam and Joshua live. I try to imagine meeting Joshua again, but Adam's face comes in between.

Later, I lean back and lower the seat. I drift off.

I wake up in Gander, Newfoundland. All I can see out the window are plateaus of grey and white, like the landscape of some unearthly planet. The stewardess explains that we must refuel here and only then fly on to London.

Soon we're soaring once again. Flying is a unique experience. In one sense you're as free as a bird because you've escaped the monotone of daily life, your obligations, and the constraints imposed by your family. In another sense, you are hostage to the engine's state of health and are expected to walk on clouds if anything goes wrong.

Too bad humans can't fly.

The couple next to me is sleeping.

Suddenly the young man turns his head toward me, and his eyes open wide. His mouth is open too, and I can smell his garlic breath. He stares at me dully at first, then smiles in recognition. I smile back. His partner lights a cigarette. I am engulfed by the cigarette fumes that drift toward me. The woman holds the cigarette loosely between her long fingers. Her nails are the colour of old blood.

I am getting restless and anxious. The couple tell me they are going to be married. They order martinis. Soon they're giggling and sleeping intermittently. I too fall asleep eventually and when I wake up, I hear the pilot announce that we'll be landing in London in thirty minutes and that it's ten o'clock in the morning.

The couple are busily arranging their things. I envy them. They have so much to look forward to. A new life ahead. But so do I.

The Awakening

The airport in London resembles a huge bazaar. Millions of people, newsstands, shops, and places to eat.

I pick up my suitcase and walk through a "British Subjects No Declaration" exit.

I see him! He's waving a bouquet of red roses. A friendly face in a mob of strangers.

He comes toward me, hands me the red roses and takes my case. Then he puts it down and gives me a bear hug. Something that I could not yet name stirs inside me, something I had first felt in Qualicum.

We weave through the crowd toward the exit. I follow his strong frame as he moves briskly down the stairs into a train station.

"We're taking the tube," says Tadeusz, in English.

"What's a tube?"

"It's a train, mostly underground, connecting the different areas of London, and the suburbs. We're going to the renowned Victoria Station."

Soon we're speeding along, chatting in Polish. He talks about the upcoming publication of my translations of Andrzej Mur's poems. I could become a famous translator. I would get a hundred pounds sterling to start, and then royalties as the book sold. There is a reading arranged in a week's time at a hall in Bloomsbury. Andrzej Mur will read the Polish, after which I will deliver the English versions.

I am overwhelmed. Tad puts his arm around me, and the familiarity of this moment seems perfect.

We arrive at Victoria Station and walk outside. I love this city. I've read so much literature that describes its history and culture. The literature of Byron, Shakespeare, Blake, Wordsworth, Eliot and, the best of all, Dickens. Of course, London is much different now than it was in Dickens' time. But one can still see a quaint country church and the seventeenth-century cottage from the train.

We take a cab to Tadeusz's apartment. London cabs are all Rolls-Royces. The front, next to the driver, has no seat and is meant for luggage. There is a glass partition between the front and the back of the cab, separating the rider from the driver. You slide open the glass door to give him instructions. The driver, who wears a uniform, is courteous and attentive. So different from my experience with North American cab drivers.

Tad talks about class distinctions. The aristocratic elite and the working class. Your trade, education, and class background define you here, much more than in Canada.

We drive into a street barely wide enough for one car.

A passerby has to squeeze through between the car door and the building's stucco wall. We park and enter a well-aged building. Tadeusz opens the door to the apartment with a very long brass key. He refers to the apartment as his "flat."

It's decorated in beige and brown with maroon, velvet-textured wallpaper. Pictures of horses and ships hang on the wall. A faded Persian runner blushes red in a brown wood-panelled hallway.

The place seems deserted. "Where are your parents?" I ask.

"My father's on vacation from his job at the Polish embassy, so they've gone to Poland, to visit relatives. So you'll stay here for a while. You want to see London, and the people connected with the reading. Don't you?"

Of course I do. I am bewildered by all this. His father must be an important person, but I also feel uncomfortable to be staying with this man, who is still, after all, a stranger. I had assumed that I would stay with his parents! This is definitely not what I'd imagined. Perhaps I should go stay with Dorothea instead. I can hear Mama's voice insisting that I phone Cousin Lola right away and go stay there, where they can keep an eye on me. But I'm finally away from their constraints and I hesitate. I'm too intrigued by all this, and now too involved.

"Don't brood," Tad says, as if reading my thoughts. "There is a special room for you here."

The flat is a one-bedroom suite with a library and a room off the kitchen.

"You can sleep in the main bedroom, and I will sleep

here," says Tad, surveying the itsy room as if he saw it for the first time. "It's the housekeeper's room, but I don't have a housekeeper," he adds, seeing my puzzled look.

"Well, you do now," I reply firmly. "I will not take away your bedroom. I like this little room, and besides, I will cook from time to time, and wash up the dishes. Don't expect waitressing though. I am really bad at it."

Tad laughs. He must have remembered the Qualicum incident.

I want to be useful. To repay his kindness. I envision the displeased look on the faces of Mama and, in particular, Max.

Tad agrees. Before long, I have the place dusted, the teakettle on, the dishes washed, and toast and marmalade on the table.

We sit and talk in the low light of a crystal lamp. Tad offers me port. I decline. He is drinking Scotch, which brings a blush to his cheeks and crystalline beads to his forehead.

"It's time to turn in," I say, feeling tired after the long trip. Tad brings over his own blue quilt to keep me warm. He kisses me ever so lightly on the cheek, then the forehead, then the lips. I turn liquid. Something stirs inside me, strong, compelling. I want to kiss him, and it's hard to stay cool. But the image of Mama intrudes, prevails. I pull away shyly, and retreat to my room. Breathe. Breathe.

Whenever something emotional like this happens to me, my first reaction is to write in my workbook. Soleil, my diary with sunflowers on it, was full of all my hidden thoughts and feelings. In this new workbook, I try to turn my experiences into poems and stories. But I don't know the end of this story yet, or even the middle. I make an entry called "The Skylark," and think of a great opening sentence which the book on writing calls "the hook."

> I wonder what the skylark sings
> when he soars toward the sky
> so joyful and free
> how I'd like to fly
> to be free like a bird
> to love, be loved and to sing.

Some hook. This is more of a silly song than a story. If only I weren't so sentimental! Though it feels good to have written about how I really feel.

I lie on the "housekeeper's bed," feeling each spring, but more than anything I feel the warmth of Tad's quilt hugging me. And even more than that, I feel the excitement of an adventure still ahead and freedom fluttering out of its cracked shell.

The six roses, which I had placed in a glass jar, are the last things I see and smell.

The next morning over breakfast, Tad announces that he is working on a story on Andrzej Mur, who fought in the Polish underground during the war and is considered a hero even by the Communists. Also, that we must hurry to an appointment with Mur later this morning.

So soon! But I have to face the reason I'm here in the first place. I haven't even telephoned Dorothea yet. What if this Mur asks me to translate some more poems? Here there is no Geoffrey White to look over my translations. Would I dare ask Tad?

I eat my breakfast while we take turns reading out loud from a volume of Canadian poetry, both English and French. My gift to Tad.

We discuss F. R. Scott, A. M. Klein, also Anne Hébert and Gatien Lapointe, poets who Tad thinks share a certain spirituality with Polish émigrés.

"It's interesting," he remarks, "to see how Canada is influenced by three cultures—American and British, with the French in the middle. "The English Canadian poetry," he muses, "reflects Canada and its hugeness.

"The French, on the other hand," Tad goes on, "see Canadian nature as an integral part of their soul. I would like to write an article on this subject."

Tad's observations are fascinating. I'd never thought of Canadian poetry in such diverse and romantic terms. I must, I promise myself, take a poetry course when and if I ever go to university.

Tad's desk is piled with newspapers. Most of them are English, some American, and others Polish. He reads them studiously. There is something mysterious about him, even harsh at times. Something both romantic and military at the same time.

He inspires and excites my imagination. How I have longed for a Polish friend. Someone with whom I can share the language I have almost forgotten. I put off calling Dorothea and Max's cousins. But what if my folks at home find out from their cousin Lola that I haven't done it yet and am nowhere to be found? It's all so scary and wonderful at the same time. I can't leave here. Not just yet. Tadeusz has opened my eyes to the literary world and a life I did not know existed.

I shower and take special care in dressing for the appointment with Mur. My beige suit and black blouse look decent in Tad's old-fashioned elliptical mirror, with its gold frame and cherubs all around.

Mur lives close by, so we walk down the Strand and through Trafalgar Square till we come to his flat.

He opens the door himself, and greets us in English, but soon turns to Polish.

"And this is Slava Lenska, your translator," says Tad.

Mur kisses my hand.

"*Enchanté*," he says in French, smiling. Is he being sarcastic, I wonder, unused to such gallantry. I know that this was definitely the European thing to do and say. He acts as if I were some grande dame, which of course I am not. I only know of such grandiosity from the Alexandre Dumas novel, *The Three Musketeers*. Now, if I were Dorothea, my aristocratic friend, that would be different.

Mur observes me with penetrating eyes. They have a light of their own but reflect a shade of distrust. He is fiftyish, of medium height, wearing a maroon dressing gown over black trousers. His hair is grey mixed with dark, and wild around his face, like the hair of a symphony conductor I had seen at a concert in Vancouver. He is a poetic version of a younger Ignace Paderewski, the acclaimed Polish pianist, composer, and politician.

Standing next to these two men, I feel like a silly teenager.

He invites us into "the salon," which in Canada is simply a living room.

"Thank you," says Mur in Polish, "for your excellent translations. Good translations are rare; only a poet should attempt to translate poetry." That's exactly what Tad had said in Qualicum. Qualicum now seems a remote village at the end of the world.

We sit at a small round table on clawed legs. A middle-aged woman brings in a china teapot with blue flowers, cups and saucers, and a tray of biscuits and sandwiches.

"It's my housekeeper, Janina," Mur explains. "Would you pour, Mademoiselle?" he asks.

I don't mind. I begin the tea-pouring ceremony I had learned at boarding school.

I feel the awkwardness easing. The two men talk about the poetry reading next week, ignoring me completely. I sip my tea, listening to every word.

"You know, Mademoiselle," Mur turns toward me, "that you will be reading the English, while I read the Polish version, so may I suggest we practise right now?"

I agree.

He tells me to stand in front of the fireplace, with Tad as our audience. We begin to read. He first, I, second.

"You read too fast, Mademoiselle," he says impatiently. "Let us do it again." We do it several more times. Mur is tough and demanding and makes this a harrowing experience. "Don't you have a strong conviction about what you are reading?" he barks.

"But I do," I reply, feeling attacked.

"Faith is the bread of the soul. You have to cultivate it

until you know the dough is ready for its destiny. Knead faith into your voice, Mademoiselle."

As I consciously try to "knead faith" into my voice, I can't help noticing that Tad's eyes are fixed on me through the entire ordeal.

We do this till dinner. Mur offers variations on my translation, and, though I feel a bit put down, it's nothing I can't handle.

Before we leave, Tad and Mur drink almost a whole bottle of Scotch, while I stuff myself with roast beef sandwiches.

Laundered mentally and physically, my wrung-out body lags behind Tad all the way to his flat. Once inside, I say good night and go to my room and to bed.

Tired as I am, I can't sleep. I get up, put on my robe and open the door. The light is on in the kitchen.

"Hello there!" exclaims Tad, who is standing by the gas stove frying some eggs. "Join me," he says simply.

I sit down at the kitchen table laid with bread, cheese, preserves, and wine.

"I'm sorry. I didn't even ask you if you were hungry. You seemed very tired." Tad places some scrambled eggs in front of me and pours me a little glass of red wine.

"Come on, girl, you need nourishment," he urges, lighting a candle on the table. "Kitchens are not that great to look at," he says, and turns off the overhead light.

Tad seems to be able to drink quite a lot of alcohol and not get drunk. I take a sip of wine, and then another. Everything in my head begins to dance and I feel warm all over.

After eating I feel stronger. Tad puts on Chopin waltzes and sits down closer, right next to me.

"You looked beautiful this afternoon, and your manners were impeccable," he says gently.

"Do you think that Mur likes my translations?" I ask, ignoring the compliment.

"Why do you have to change the subject? Listen, Mur is lucky to have someone like you translate his work. He has but a small audience here in London, and none in North America. You may have opened doors for him."

I am satisfied.

There is an uneasy silence in the room.

"Let's dance," says Tad.

We dance the whole record through. Slowly. Close. Suddenly, a Polish Polka bursts out of the record player. We dance so fast I can barely breathe. When it ends, we fall onto the couch.

Tad starts to kiss me and I let him. My body turns liquid. His hand strokes my hair ever so softly, then my face. Everything disappears, my thoughts, the room. In the next moment I return his kisses. Our clothed bodies melt together. I reach out to caress his neck and back. I feel his fingers fumbling with my robe, beneath which I am naked. It slips off my shoulders. Tad's breath is on my skin. I panic. I have never gone this far. Mama's voice echoes in my head. "No," she warns. "Don't. Don't!"

With difficulty I pull away and jump up, dragging my robe.

Tad stares at me with disbelief. "We shouldn't..." His voice breaks off.

"No," I reply weakly and go back to my room. I lay down on my bed still feeling Tad's closeness. The six red roses he gave me are fiery red now, and their scent heady. Didn't someone once tell me that red is the color of passion?

The Triumph and the Failure

The next day, I telephone Dorothea.

Even though I want to see her, I am relieved to find out that she is away for a few days. The world I am in now cannot be interrupted. It is filled with poetry and Tad.

I am no longer the childlike Slava of Montreal, or the struggling Elizabeth at boarding school in Victoria. Tad seems a little detached at times and I feel insecure about his feelings for me. Adam, from this vantage point, is but a pin on the map of my life. Joshua is still there, like a sunflower in my grandfather's garden which I loved but now exists only in memory.

I've been spending a lot of time with Mur while Tad is away on his own business, about which he seems very secretive. Mur and I share the poetry of Émile Nelligan. The French Canadian poet was only seventeen years old and writing profound verse. I can understand enough French to see the similarity between his work and the poetry of Arthur Rimbaud, the French poet. Nelligan's

Poésies Complètes came out just this year.

Mur particularly likes "Le Vaisseau D'or"—"The Ship Of Gold." I argue that the section called "Le Jardin de L'enfance"—"The Childhood Garden" is better.

He teaches me a lot about poetry. He explains a literary movement called *Les Imagistes*, which is led by an American poet, Ezra Pound. In their 1915 manifesto, the Imagists vowed to strip poetry to its bare essentials, no more rhyme or frilly and flowery expressions, only concrete, clear metaphors unencumbered by verbosity.

What a revelation! My own poetry rhymes, and sounds hopelessly out of date. It's full of nostalgia. But inspired now by everything around me, I begin to write new poems, different ones, using what the Imagists called *le vers libre:* free verse.

Tad says they're good, but need pruning. I don't have enough confidence to show my new work to Mur.

The Sunday afternoon of the reading finally arrives. Mur and Tad have bought me a red velvet dress for the occasion. My hair, sun-streaked with blonde, is now curlier due to London's dampness.

I look at myself in Tad's mirror, and see a very pretty young woman in a red dress and low-heeled black shoes, with a slim straight body and shapely legs. There is a glow to her face and eyes. What has become, I wonder, of Slava, and Elizabeth? There are no visible traces of the war child or the immigrant girl in this glamorous eighteen-year-old. The two seem to have merged into this new image. But is this new person really me? What would Mama say, not to mention Max? I bet Dorothea won't even recognize me. I have left a message with their house-keeper informing Dorothea of the time and place of the reading. I hope she comes.

The hall is filling up with people. Some elegantly dressed, others simply. The poets sit in the front row on the right side, their translators in the front row on the left.

Tadeusz stands in front of a microphone trying to get the crowd's attention. He cuts an imposing figure, tall and elegant in his dark jacket, grey pants and red-striped tie. The audience grows quiet. Tad begins to speak. His voice is loud and smooth. He introduces the first poet and her translator. The poet is Hungarian. The next one is Russian, then German, then our turn comes.

My head feels light. Detached from my body. We walk toward our respective lecterns. Mur begins to read his poem in Polish. I think I see Dorothea sitting in the back row. Mur stops reading. There is silence, which I must break. I begin to recite my English translation of Mur's poem. I try to put substance into my voice, but it strikes a hollow. Get on with it! I remember Mur's "bread" and feel hot. It's hard to be emotional. But these poems! They speak of exile and longing for one's homeland. I think of my own distorted sense of belonging and a voice starts to come from a deep place in my throat.

After Mur and I finish reading, people stand up and clap.

Dorothea runs over, accompanied by her chauffeur. We embrace and excitedly examine each other from head to toe. She seems taller and even more beautiful than at

Qualicum. I introduce her to Tad and Mur, who are now surrounded by people offering their congratulations.

Afterwards, there is a reception at Mur's flat. Dorothea and I drink punch. Mur thanks me and presents me with a bouquet of orange-red roses. He tells me that the honorarium for my translations will be sent to me.

Dorothea leaves, promising to phone me tomorrow to arrange a meeting. She seems puzzled that I am not staying with her. As she leaves with her handsome chauffeur, everyone's eyes turn and follow them out the door.

Tadeusz comes over to join me and doesn't leave my side even for a moment. Being near him feels safe and good. I think that what I feel for him may be the real thing. Does he feel the same way about me?

Vancouver seems far away in the past. London is thrilling. After the reception, Tadeusz and I walk in St. James' Park, Trafalgar Square, the Strand. We end up in Tad's flat, where we spend the evening. We try to be as close as before, but I can't help feeling a distance growing between us.

The next afternoon Mur invites us to Banbury for tea. I am just about to devour my aromatic Banbury bun when a group of people wanders in. Among them, immediately noticeable, is a beautiful woman with an upswept hairdo, wearing a snow-white dress that sharply contrasts with her huge brown eyes and tanned skin.

Almost immediately she makes her way toward Tad. He sees her and turns a shade paler. She approaches and kisses him on the cheek.

"This is Marysia Kotar," says Tad nervously. "An old

friend." The woman smiles like the Mona Lisa in one of my art books.

"I just flew in from Warsaw," she says excitedly. "I tried to call you but no answer. I am here on a visit scavenging for cheap versions of fashionable British dresses and suits for Poland. You know how our stores have nothing." She continues to bend over Tad, who spills his tea. So out of character. Does he really like this woman? The thought makes me sick.

"It was by special order of our party supervisor that I was able to come," she whispers in his ear, but we can hear. Tad absentmindedly promises to call her. He has her phone number, he says. "All visitors from the Eastern bloc stay at this one hotel, which is watched by party members," he tells us after she leaves to join her group at another table. Tad shifts around in his chair restlessly, and, like a small child in a playpen, looks wistfully over at Marysia.

In the meantime, my world collapses. I hardly know what to think. This older sophisticated woman, and a greenhorn like me. I feel jealous and resentful all the way home, and start to regret allowing myself to become so close to Tad. I desperately want to return to his flat to clear the air.

"I know how you feel, Slava," he replies later when I confront him. "This woman and I were very much in love once, but because of my work we separated. I told her that she was free to see other men. There have been other women in my life.

"I like you, Slava, very much, but I am not one to get

tied down to anyone. In my work, I need to be free."

It's as if a giant paw with claws were entering my body and churning my insides. Hating myself for my stupidity, my naiveté, I get up to go to my room, and hold my breath. He neither stops nor follows me.

I sit in my room for a long time. The phone rings. Tad answers. I listen by the door.

"Servus Andrzej," says Tad in Polish. "Yes, we need to meet to discuss our trip to Warsaw." He continues, "I must leave in two weeks at the latest. Coming with me? You'll be a good deal safer. OK, old man. See you tomorrow." End of conversation. The door bangs shut. I peer out into the hall and see that Tad's jacket is gone from the hat stand.

What on earth were they talking about?

My bleak private world returns, crowned by memories of war and its aftermath. Old images spring to mind: of being an immigrant in Canada, underprivileged, poor, the outsider. Is the fairy tale over so soon? But I don't want to go back to being the person I was before all this happened.

I can't and I won't. I must find out where I belong in this world, and not be an object blown by the wind. There must be a definite reason for my being here.

Why didn't I know they were planning a trip to Warsaw?

Anger and bitterness engulf all my previous feelings for Tadeusz. I decide not to spend another night here. I telephone Dorothea. Hearing the depression in my voice, she immediately invites me to come and stay with her, even offers to send a car for me within an hour. I pack my things helter-skelter and am about to leave when the phone rings.

I answer reluctantly. It's Andrzej Mur. I tell him that Tadeusz has gone out for the evening. He is silent for a moment. "I know," he answers. "I spoke with him. Tomorrow I would like to speak with you. I'll come and get you. We'll go somewhere for tea."

"I'll be staying with a girlfriend," I say, curious about the appointment he has with Tad but reluctant to ask. Mur is no fool. He must know something is up. But I have come to love and trust the man, so I give him Dorothea's telephone number and address.

I telephone Max's cousin. They sound worried. They've been waiting for my call. Where have I been? Mama and Max have written them that I was coming to London, and forwarded a letter for me in a large envelope. When can I come and stay with them?

I am intrigued about the letter, but I tell them that I am staying with my girlfriend from St. Anne's School and can come only the next day.

Lola listens. Her response is curt. Do I detect suspicion in her voice?

5
Fate

A grey Rolls-Royce is waiting in front of Tad's building.

"Good evening to you, miss," says the chauffeur, helping me with my luggage.

I settle back against the luxurious leather cushioning of the seats and embark on what seems like a long drive, gazing distractedly at the quaintness of London. I stare into the red double-decker buses searching people's faces. They bear the look of ordinary citizens going about their ordinary business of life. Who can really know what truth lurks behind their calm exteriors?

We stop in front of an elegant mansion surrounded by a park.

Dorothea runs out to greet me. She is absolutely gorgeous in a sleeveless black linen dress that clings to her shapely body. Her hair is styled into a sophisticated short blond bob that frames her small face. Her blue eyes effervesce with violet light.

"Liz, welcome. How wonderful you look!" she

51

exclaims, hugging me.

We walk into the house arm in arm. It is magnificent. High ceilings with frescoes in blues, yellows, and oranges. Period furniture, but which period, I wonder? There are carved Oriental pieces, vases, and sculptures. Carpets with exotic patterns line floors that shine like glass.

Dorothea insists that I unpack and rest briefly before tea. The butler takes my suitcase upstairs to a room all done up in blue. There is a vase of red and pink carnations on the shiny mahogany desk with a card that says:

WELCOME TO BLUEFORT MANOR

Love

Dorothea and family

I unpack. Out comes Papa's photograph, and, at the very bottom of the suitcase, I come across the red file. I'd forgotten all about it. I sit down at the desk and decide to read it quickly.

I thumb through the photographs once again, then launch into the other pages. The first one is handwritten. I concentrate on the Polish:

I, Stefan Lenski, accuse Roman Mortynski, formerly my best friend, of blackmail.

That said Mortynski blackmailed my mother, Katya Lenska, exchanging my daughter's life for money and disclosure of my hiding place. He threatened that if she didn't comply, he would inform the Nazis on my older daughter, Slava, who was then hiding with my mother in the care of Vladislav Lipa. Mortynski also warned my mother that the Gestapo would torture

Slava until she gave away my address.

Therefore, in danger, hunted by the Nazis, I had to come out of hiding to meet with Mortynski to ensure Slava's safety. The meeting was arranged by my mother at her home.

Said Mortynski then proceeded to extort property from me in exchange for the life of my younger daughter, Basia, whom I had smuggled out of the dangers of the Warsaw ghetto and given into his safekeeping. He claimed that the property I was to sign over to him would bribe the Gestapo into saving Basia's life. He said that Basia, after she was informed on and taken by the Gestapo, was held in a convent until the ransom the Nazis were promised for her life was paid. After my mother and I had given him what he wanted, both the money and the property, he informed me that Basia had already been murdered. He did not return what he took from me, not my daughter, not my property, nor my mother's money.

Said Mortynski eventually gave me away to the Gestapo, revealing to them the address of my residence in a Polish village where my wife and I were hiding.

I also accuse Mortynski of being a blackmailer, on the grounds that he extracted money from other Jewish people in hiding, such as M. Richtman of Falenica, and made a business out of their misery.

I accuse him of having collaborated with the Nazis, on the grounds that he promised them money, which he extorted from my family, while he himself went unharmed for hiding a Jewish child for which the Nazi punishment was death.

Finally, right after the war, Mortynski came after me a number of times with a revolver, and threatened to kill me and harm my children. He was the main reason that I fled Poland with my family immediately afterwards.

There follows a list of names of families Mortynski was said to have blackmailed, and many more pages of typewritten legal material. There is a document stating that Papa's suit against Mortynski was rejected by the Polish court for lack of evidence, and that my grandmother's and her friend Vlad's testimony in support of my father's accusations was rejected on the grounds of "supreme subjectivity."

Next come handwritten scraps of paper containing Father's rebuttal and re-appeal. But they aren't finished, and are dated close to the day he died. Looking at these papers, written toward the end of Papa's life, I can see how the strength of his writing had declined in step with his failing health.

On yet another crumpled piece of paper, Father had written the following:

While still in Poland I heard rumours that Mortynski was a Nazi collaborator. My wife and I suspect that he had saved our daughter's life but didn't want to return her to us after the war.

I never really learned the truth about what happened to my daughter Basia, and in what sequence. The only proof of her death was offered to me by Mortynski, in 1944. He took me to her so-called place

of burial (it wasn't a proper grave) and showed me
legs clothed in socks and shoes. How could I have
known whether they were really hers?

They could have been anyone's, I think to myself, over-
come with dread. No wonder my parents continued to
look for Basia after the war.

There are also three documents attesting to my father's
ownership of several properties, including an apartment
building in Warsaw, and the Rose Villa in Malinow.
Property lost to us, stolen by Mortynski. Property that
could have made a big difference in our lives: to think
that we would not have had to struggle so hard as immigrants if we had our property. Maybe Papa wouldn't have
had to work so hard at the deli and gotten sick. Maybe we
could have owned a home.

And the man who stole it, Mortynski, goes unpun-
ished. He remains the false owner of what today could
well have been ours. One hope remains: he didn't get the
Rose Villa, which is still in my grandfather's name. Only
now it probably belongs to the Communist government
of Poland.

I stare at the proof of my inheritance, and see only
worn sheets of paper, held together by rusted staples.

I flip through several more pages of the file, and, at the
very end, I find Papa's drawing of lilies of the valley and
his poem below it. The lilies are perfectly drawn. Little
bells on pale green stems nestling inside the gentle leaves.
I can almost smell them, they are so real. The poem
brings back bittersweet memories.

I translate it into English:

Lilies of the Valley
For my two daughters, Slava and Basia

Lilies of the valley, fragrant bells
Infant faces on lithe stems
Subtle miniatures, shimmering like stars
Like the innocent eyes of little girls
Gorgeous white bonnets over green capes
Lifting their heads toward warmth, toward the sun
Sisterly souls, golden sunbeams
You strain your arms toward your absent parents
Flutter white bells, ring out wistful and tender
While the wind bends your heads and clouds hide the sun
But wait! When the wind dies and the sun awakens
I will gather you into a bouquet once again
And hold you close to my heart.

Papa

*Written by Stefan Lenski on Christmas Day, 1943
while in hiding from the Nazis in a Polish village,
separated from his two young daughters, who were in
hiding elsewhere.*

The contents of this file enter my being. I am back there again. The little girl whose body would freeze up so often against the frosty wall of ice and snow outside the window of our house. Against the nightmarish wall of the Warsaw ghetto. Against the wall of tears of abandoned children, crying for their Mama and Papa.

The past returns, wearing a ghost-mask.

It's two-sided. On one side is Slava, the helpless little

girl in hiding, praying for the safety of her sister and parents. On the other is Elizabeth, the Canadian teenager making her way in the world. Up till now I had almost thought that Slava had disappeared for good. Instead she has returned, forcing me to go back there again. Once again I feel like two people, two links on a chain of life, one here, another there, connected only by the string of memory, knotted into a file and a few black and white photographs.

The question remains: will I ever find Basia and get the Rose Villa back? Must I take on responsibility for my father's unfinished business? If not I, the eldest child, then who?

I wish Papa were here to tell me what to do. Instead he just smiles at me from a photograph on the desk.

The maid announces that tea will be served in the library in five minutes. I try to pull myself together.

Downstairs, I sink into more plush leather. Tea is served by a red-cheeked, plump maid wearing a black dress and white apron. A white eyelet cotton cap perches crookedly on her head.

"My parents are away in Cannes," says Dorothea, "so we have the house to ourselves." She pauses then continues. "What's the matter, Liz, you look so awfully pale?"

I shrug my shoulders, unwilling to go into detail about what I have just read.

We talk into the night. She tells me that she is deeply in love with a philosophy student at Cambridge and that they plan to marry when they both finish university. She is studying English literature at Oxford.

I loosen up and tell her my latest news. From the translations, to being with Tad, to Papa's file.

"Tadeusz reminds me of my stepfather, the Earl of Roxford. A typical womanizer!" Dorothea says adamantly. I am sure she is right. That's what Tad is, a stupid womanizer! But he has also brought me to London, I argue, and respects my translations. Surely there is more to him than just womanizing?

Dorothea slowly picks up on the file. She wants to see it. We run upstairs and go over it together. Dorothea is beside herself with excitement. "Liz, you and your past never cease to amaze me," she exclaims.

"I have an idea! What if you went with Tad and Mur to Poland?" Dorothea is almost shouting. "To try to find your sister and this man, Mortynski. This could be a great opportunity for you. Grab it! I know how you've always anguished over Basia. Over the war. Maybe this will help you to come to terms with these things."

It was almost like listening to Miriam in the old days in Montreal. Every time I was fumbling in the dark, Miriam was able to set me on the right path.

It had never occurred to me to go to Warsaw with Mur and Tad.

Maybe there is something called fate. Maybe everything that has happened up till now followed a pattern of some higher order that was beyond human understanding. But how can I trust Tad now? We both decide that I must take a chance.

Dorothea and I devise a plan. It's a long shot but it may work. We decide to drive back to Tad's flat, and leave the file for him to find "accidentally."

The ride to Tad's place seems unending. I am hoping that he hasn't returned home. His windows are dark. The car waits for us as we walk stealthily up to the flat. I turn the key in the door and peer into the corridor. We creep in, holding our breath. The flat is steeped in darkness and silence, punctuated by the slow ticking of the clock.

Dorothea keeps vigil by the window while I place the red file on the top of the dresser in the housekeeper's room. Tadeusz is bound, we figure, to check this room when he comes home and finds me gone.

"Hurry, hurry," says Dorothea. We rush down, our feet sounding hollow on the wooden staircase, then dash into the street and the car.

Just as we drive around the corner, Tad's car goes by. I think I see a woman sitting in the front seat. It's that Marysia Kotar!

On the one hand, I feel glad that I left my file for Tad. On the other, I worry. What if it gets lost? If Tad never sees it or just throws it out?

Mama used to say that fate has to be accompanied by a little bit of mazel: good luck.

6 Mazel

Once again I am on a plane, this time to Warsaw, Poland.

I feel like a lark soaring, until the back of my seat plunges me forward to reality. It's broken. A wingless bird, I rock back and forth until the turbulence stops.

Many of the people on this airline speak Polish. I also hear Russian spoken.

Tadeusz and Mur are discussing poetry and politics. I eavesdrop and learn that in London, Paris, and even Warsaw, poets and novelists gather in cafés and discuss their art, even read it out loud. In Russia, poets enjoy a privileged life and large audiences.

This is so different from the attitude in Vancouver, where some of the people I know, including Adam, think writing poetry is a sissy's hobby. Tad is a paradoxical combination of politician and poet, and is anything but a sissy.

Tad and Mur talk on, completely ignoring me, as usual. The plane rocks and shakes. I think of Mama and

Max, and Pyza. What if I crash? No one will ever know what happened to me. I think of Papa and try to find strength. I must, so that my mind won't give in to fear and self-pity. For comfort, I turn to the most immediate memory.

Dorothea and I visited Max's cousins in Hampstead. They seemed kind and hospitable. I explained where I was staying, and they were puzzled, but impressed with Dorothea and her "address" in the fashionable district of Mayfair.

While they seemed pleasant enough, I knew that I would not have been comfortable there. They were old-fashioned like Max. Lola handed me an envelope. There was a letter of reprimand from Mother and Max, wondering why they hadn't heard from me. I had only recently written them about staying with Dorothea. Our letters must have crossed. Soon after lunch we said goodbye, explaining that I would spend the rest of my visit at Dorothea's.

Just as we returned home at two o'clock, Mur phoned, offering to come and take me out to tea. I barely had time to wash up and change, glad that at least Dorothea was going riding and didn't expect me to stay with her all day.

At three o'clock sharp, Mur pulled up in front of the house in a yellow Beetle. Before I knew it we were off into the London traffic. We stopped near the British Museum, where we were to have tea.

No sooner had we walked into the cafeteria than I saw Tad sitting at one of the tables. I froze, but Mur urged me to sit down at the same table. Although Tad was not a person I cared to see today, I felt anxious about the Lenski File.

"I know that this is a surprise for you," said Mur, discerningly. "I arranged it, kill me if you wish." I did feel like killing somebody, but not literally, because I even found it difficult to kill a daddy-long-legs crawling in the bathtub. Obviously Tad had told Mur what had happened and Mur wanted to make peace between us.

Tad kissed me on the cheek tenderly as if nothing had happened, asked how I was and handed me a parcel. Inside a brown paper bag was a familiar object—my red file.

He had found it after all!

"You left this open on top of your bureau," he said, looking at me with a puzzled expression. "When I saw all your things gone, I searched inside this folder for some clues to your disappearance. Forgive me, Slava, but I was desperate to cast some light on what was going on with you. When I read what was in it, I became unhinged. Thank God good old Mur telephoned soon afterwards and told me where you had gone."

I was beginning to feel more benevolent toward Tad. He sounded as though he meant what he was saying. Tad continued, "Slava, tell Andrzej about this file. You can trust him. He is anti-Nazi and anti-Communist. He fought with the Underground during the war, and eventually escaped through Russia to England on a cargo boat. He understands what the Jews went through during the war. He has written about the pogrom in Kielce."

I told Mur something about myself, while Tad, who already knew everything, quietly listened. I told him about the war, my father, Basia, Mortynski and black-mail, and The Rose Villa. He listened carefully, particularly to the story about Basia.

"I don't know why I even brought this file," I mumbled, feeling helpless about the whole situation.

"Pure intuition," said Mur.

"What do you mean?" I queried.

"I have a proposal for you," he stated firmly. "In a week, I am going to Poland to read at the University of Warsaw. I've written some papers on Socialist Realism, a literary movement in Russia started by Maxim Gorky, whose work I translated into Polish. Tadeusz, I know, also has to go back, as his time in London is up."

A miracle was happening. Mazel had arrived at my life's gates.

"I didn't know that," I commented weakly, pretending ignorance. "Tad is full of secrets," I added maliciously. The two men looked at one another.

"Listen to me," continued Mur. "You can travel as my assistant. I have connections at the University of Warsaw. What do you say?"

Tadeusz intervened. "It would be better if Slava came as my assistant," he said. "I am a member of the Communist Party in good standing, and have some pull." Then he whispered, "Ask Mur, he knows all about me."

"Yes," said Mur. "He's right. It would be better if you went as Tad's assistant. He works for the Polish government, so it is easier for him to get the permits. They trust him over there."

More unbelievable revelations about Tad!

Now the thought of going back to Poland was frightening and at the same time exhilarating. My life always seemed to have two opposite elements fighting like old soldiers, each in a different landscape. I longed to see the sunflower gardens once more, the fields of wheat, and sunlit meadows. To pick wild berries in fern-dense forests. To find traces of my lost childhood in the city of my birth. All these made my visit seem like a return to a paradise once lost and now found.

But there loomed the shadows of a terrible past with all its dark remembrances. And what about the politics of Poland, its Communist regime in which the people had no freedom, were spied on and constrained. And myself, a foreigner and a Jew?

The more I thought of it, the more frightened I became. But an inner voice informed me that I had no choice, that I had to go and tend to my family's unfinished business.

I vaguely heard Mur agreeing with Tad. Hardly knowing what I was saying, I agreed to go. My mind became a transparent vessel travelling through space. It seemed that I had entered a moment or a place in time from which there could be no turning back.

It was decided that, a week from today, the three of us would leave for Warsaw.

"But while we're making arrangements for our departure, we must design a plan of attack. How and where to find Mortynski, and the addresses of your properties," noted Tad.

"I think I have them somewhere in these notes," I said.

Shortly after, Mur left me alone with Tadeusz.

"I'll take you home," he offered, "but first let's talk." I couldn't very well refuse, though I was nervous about what he had to say.

"Slava," began Tadeusz, "I can only tell you that I am sorry. I do care for you, but not in the way of 'I will love you forever.'" There it was again. Deflation.

"Please believe that I didn't mean to take advantage of you. You're still too young emotionally to handle this type of relationship. Besides, I live in Poland and you live in Canada..." Tad paused.

What did he mean, "this type of a relationship"? Just because I was only eighteen was no reason to assume that I could not love a man. But I couldn't speak. Instead, I grew silent and frozen as in the days of old, like a glacier in the Arctic.

"I want to make it up to you by doing everything I can to help you find your sister," Tad continued.

I still cared for Tad, but I decided to put my disap-- pointment aside. Trying to find Basia was the closest thing to my heart right now. We knew so little about her. How could I live with myself if I let this opportunity pass by?

On the other hand, Tadeusz was a playboy and a communist. Earlier, while Tad was in the washroom, Mur quickly told me that Tad worked for the secret police in the field of cultural censorship and everything involving the press, radio, and film. He reported to Polish authorities about cultural events in London and the latest news in the western press. Tadeusz was watched by plainclothes men from the party. They didn't trust anybody, and checked on him inconspicuously from time to time. Though I pride myself on being very observant, I hadn't noticed anyone following us.

I definitely didn't trust Tadeusz as much as I trusted Mur. I asked myself questions and more questions. Should I notify Mama and Max about this? Did I want to take this giant step without them knowing? How could I go to a country that had never been well disposed toward the Jewish people?

I decided to talk it over with Dorothea. She was bubbling with excitement because our plan had worked, but she was also trying to place the whole thing in a clearer perspective.

"This is the problem, as I see it. First of all, your parents would never allow you to do such a thing," she said, outlining the idea with two fingers. "Secondly, you're going as your father's eldest daughter on a family mission he was unable to fulfil. I don't know much about Poland," she continued, "but isn't it a communist country, and dangerous?" Inwardly, I knew she was right. Of course it could be dangerous.

"I have made up my mind," I replied, sounding braver than I felt. "I am going! One thing is sure, neither my mother or my stepfather must know about this. They'd never let me go. I will tell the English cousins that I've gone with you to Cornwall or Wales for a holiday." I paused, waiting for Dorothea's response.

"That's lying, Liz. Lying doesn't work. Remember St. Anne's, my sneaking out with Joe and all the trouble that followed?" She reflected for a moment. "But I owe you one, don't I? You didn't tell on me either."

It was agreed then. I was free to do what felt best.

Now I sit back and marvel at how unexpectedly and quickly, after a mere week of talk and preparations, Tadeusz, Mur and I were able to board this plane for Warsaw.

Suddenly the broken seat catapults me forward, ejecting me out of a dream into reality. And I brace myself for what is ahead.

Red Tape

The stewardess announces our descent into Warsaw and tells us to buckle up. A lady in front of me throws up into a brown paper bag. A sour, nauseating smell pervades the cabin. Below us, Warsaw emerges out of the clouds.

We touch down in the land to which I thought I would never return—the land of my childhood and the genocide of my people. Will I find Basia here? My sunflower garden? The traces of my childhood?

We taxi along the airstrip and stop.

The plane door opens and we climb down the stairway. A strong wind hits my face and dishevels my hair. We walk along the dusty field to the central building.

The terminal is small and dark. People line up in front of the passport control wickets. There seem to be more officers than people. They ask many questions. Their faces are sour, eyes filled with suspicion. The passengers nervously juggle their documents, small cases, jackets, and whatever possessions they carry. Each person's moves are closely monitored by the officers at passport control.

I stand between Tadeusz and Mur, my new Canadian passport and Polish visa handy. Tadeusz is first. He flashes something in front of the customs officer. The officer questions him briefly, then salutes and lets him through. Tad says something, pointing back to me. The officer's smile freezes as he beckons. It's my turn.

Fear strangles my throat. I hope I don't have to speak.

Since my documents state that I was born in Warsaw, the customs officer lingers over the information. Asks me why I came here.

"I am here as an assistant to Mr. Skovronek," I reply in Polish. My memorized answer comes out better than I expected. The officer looks me over. Up, down, and sideways. Then he actually smiles and asks to see the contents of my bag. While I cringe, he rummages through some clothing, never reaching deep enough to find Papa's file.

"How much money do you have, and in what currency?" he asks in a stern voice.

"Fifty pounds sterling," I reply almost defiantly, putting on my best self-assured mask.

He doesn't comment, closes the bag and motions me through.

I breathe more freely.

Mur is behind us, and gets an even longer grilling. Two officers turn his briefcase inside out. Shuffle through his papers. They read several pages and consult another officer who shrugs his shoulders and says in Polish, "What's the difference? He has written permission to enter; if anything is not right, we'll find out soon enough. Let him through."

Tad tells me that Mur's reputation in Poland was tainted by the anti-communist poems he wrote right after the war. And he strongly disapproves of censorship, and of the kind of literature the communist system advocates: propaganda. However, as a professor in the Slavonic Department at London University he wrote a paper praising Maxim Gorky, a socialist writer. Knowing that Mur is not a communist, I wondered why he did this. Now I understand. Like every exile, he wants to return to his homeland, even if it is only for a brief visit. Even if it means exalting Gorky, who is albeit, as Mur puts it, "a good writer." In Mur's words, "a good writer can even transcend censorship."

We walk into the Polish sunshine. The wind has subsided. There is hardly anyone around in front of the terminal building. This airport, small and dingy, bears no resemblance to North American or British airports. The few people that are here seem quiet and unsmiling, observing us suspiciously.

Outside the terminal, Tadeusz hails a car that resembles a '47 Ford, and has no "taxi" sign. We climb in. The interior reeks of cigarette smoke, musk, and vegetable soup.

The driver is hatless, wearing a shirt, jacket and tie, all of which need cleaning. But he smiles at us and says in informal Polish, "You folks have dollars?"

"First, sir, drive us to the Bristol Hotel, if you please," says Tadeusz firmly.

"If you folks have two pounds," continues the driver, "we can do business. Give me two, mister, and I'll drive you all anywhere you want to go."

"How many zlotys will you give me for a pound sterling?" asks Tad.

"For one pound I can give you two hundred zlotys. You can live here for a month on that. But nobody can find out about it."

Tad makes a sign with his hand for us to give him some money.

"Isn't that illegal?" I whisper to him. Having discovered that there is a black market in Poland, I am worried—what if the secret police find out that we are getting Polish currency illegally?

"It's better than the official exchange," says Tad. We need some local currency, so Mur and I each hand Tad a couple of pounds.

"We're supposed to get currency at the government's official exchange counter at the airport. But we won't tell anyone," says Tad with a wicked grin.

What a clandestine beginning.

The Bristol is an old hotel. The carpets are the colour of faded pink roses. The long, old-fashioned windows are draped in cream-coloured sheers and yellowy satin. There are several people at the check-in counter. Tadeusz asks for two rooms with bathrooms for myself and Mur.

"We can give you two rooms," replies the concierge acidly. "But bathrooms are not available just yet, maybe you want to wait," he says, goggling at us from behind his glasses. "Your passports, please," he adds curtly, stretching out a nicotine-tainted palm. Tad slips a two-pound note into one of the passports. The concierge checks them beneath the counter. His face suddenly brightens, "I think we can find some bathrooms after all," he says with sudden joviality, handing over two keys. "Your passports will be returned to you when you check out of the hotel."

The rooms are next to one another. The beds in each are narrow, like wooden benches with mattresses on top, placed parallel to the wall.

The bathrooms are poorly lit; each has a chain hanging from the ceiling over the toilet, for flushing. The taps leak. I remember this type of bathroom in the ghetto during the war. The chain there was always broken, and excrement floated around the toilet bowl.

Through a grimy window covered with crushed dead flies, I see the Warsaw skyline. The grey buildings are mostly low and square and close together. Ruins of bombed-out buildings are still visible, although the Poles have already rebuilt many of the city's war-wounded streets. Many buildings are surrounded by scaffolding, and some are only half-formed. In between them, I can see open spaces piled with brick.

Far in the distance, I see the tall green trees of the parks I had loved as a child. The red brick of Stare Miasto, the Old City. Church steeples, looming high, dominate the city's landscape.

"Let's eat," says Mur. "I'm starved."

Tad suggests the hotel café, famous for its delicious cakes. We sit down at a small round marble table.

"Before the war," Tad reminisces, "men and women, writers and artists would gather in this café for their afternoon snacks. In those days, I would come with my parents. There was classical music here, laughter, cigarette smoke, drinks.

"The conversation revolved around politics, love, literature, music, art, and theatre. Everyone seemed in such great spirits, even in 1939, just before the Blitzkrieg." Tadeusz grows silent and sips his coffee. For a moment his face softens with memory, then in a flash his features return to the rigidity of the government security man, or *SB*, in Polish jargon.

Mur and I are quiet, lapping up every bit of it, looking around, trying to imagine the place as it must have been then, elegant and merry. But the sombre look on Mur's face reflects my own inner sadness. The war had placed a cruel stamp on this city, and on the lives of many people.

A sloppy-looking waiter comes by and throws several grease-spotted menus at us. He eyes us with contempt, and says, "No fresh meat today. On Mondays it all goes East."

"To Russia," explains Tad.

But there is bigos, which I instantly recognize. It is one of my favourite Polish dishes: sauerkraut and sausage, served with boiled potatoes and fresh black bread. We also have red wine, and for dessert, apple Charlotte.

The meal is delicious, even though the bigos was short on meat, with only a tiny bit of sausage here and there. The waiter, who had appeared sleepy and apathetic, cheers up when Tad surreptitiously slips him an illegal tip. The waiter looks furtively around, to make sure no one is watching, then quickly slips the money deep into his pocket. He is a lot nicer to us after that.

"Tips are illegal here," explains Tad. "The government calls them bribes. But, with that money, he can perhaps buy a piece of meat for his family on the black market, or maybe get his wife a new dress."

Tad excuses himself, saying that he has to go and see his relatives, with whom he is staying.

"I'll see you first thing in the morning. Don't forget, as foreign visitors you must register with the police within twenty-four hours of your arrival. I will make the necessary arrangements, but you must report in person. There's a lot of red tape for foreigners. The hotel has its own Security Department to handle these things—you can go there." He shakes hands with Mur and kisses me on both cheeks, then leaves.

Left to ourselves, Mur and I take a short walk outside. Walking on the pavement of Marshalkowska Street has a strange effect on me. I am like Alice in Wonderland. I was five when I last walked with Papa on this street, where I was born, where I met my first dog, my first disappointment, and my first joy, before everything happened.

I rewind the memory of the Blitzkrieg, the burning ghetto, the wounded city of Warsaw.

This permanent film is my vehicle for revisiting unhealed wounds.

To this day I wonder whether that wounded Russian soldier is alive or dead. Right after the war, when we were travelling through Warsaw in a horse-driven buggy, a twisted, bent body jumped in and lay at our feet like bundle of rags. He lay face down, holding his chest, blood gushing onto the cart floor and our shoes. He was wounded while fighting Germans for the city of Warsaw. And he won, losing his heart in the process. My father took him to a makeshift hospital. Two men carried him away on a stretcher. His face was ashen, his eyes closed.

"You're deep in thought," observes Mur.

Shadowy memories, momentary excerpts of those confusing and unfortunate days, crowd into my mind, like ants onto an anthill.

"Yes," I remark absentmindedly, feeling vulnerable and fragile.

"What is troubling you?" he prods.

Unable to answer, I burst into tears. Suddenly my foot catches on something and I fall forward onto my hands and knees. Mur helps me up. The passersby stare with cold eyes, sensing in us the presence of foreigners. My elbows and my knees are bruised and dirty. My stockings are in shreds. Mur leads me to the wall of a building and puts his arms around me. He comforts me and wipes away my tears with his handkerchief. For a moment he seems like Papa, and I, a mere child.

"We'd better go home now," says Mur. His face is serious. I follow his eyes toward a man standing on the corner of the street. The man is wearing a black leather coat. His eyes are fixed on us like a hawk's. I sense that he is following us as we turn the corner. We walk into the hotel and turn around. He remains on the street, still looking at us.

"That's Big Brother watching," says Mur. I don't really understand, and ask him to explain.

"He's a member of the Communist Party, making sure everyone behaves. You and I look like foreigners. They can tell. Even if we are of Polish origin. Our clothes look Western, and they don't like people like us from democratic countries that are in a cold war with the Communist bloc. Don't you know?"

"Yes, I know." I learned about it from the news on the radio and from Adam.

"You'll find that everything that seems normal in the West is either forbidden or suspect here. That's the system. It's probably forbidden to pee in yellow."

Though I laugh at Mur's remark, I am thankful that Mama and Max don't know about all this. There are hidden dangers here, and I hope I'll get out alive. Suddenly, the magic of coming back to Warsaw pales as some of my old fear from the war days returns, and I begin to look over my shoulder.

In spite of all this, I promise myself that while I am here, I must accept each day with a smile, and with a strong focus on my reason for coming—Basia.

A Different World

Smiling in Poland doesn't come easily. Mur is right. There are strict rules here, different from those in the free world.

You have to watch what you say, where, to whom. Even your furniture has ears. Mur tells me the hotel rooms may be wired for SB-security snooping, that the SB is the Polish version of the Russian KGB. Mikes can be found planted behind paintings, inside lamps or plugs. "But," says Mur, "here in Poland, rules are not as strict as in other communist countries."

People in the streets and stores appear serious and watchful, as they did at the Warsaw airport. Yesterday I saw lineups at the butcher shop and the dairy. The newspaper is full of propaganda against the West. Magazines push industry and agriculture rather than fashion and the arts. The stores are almost empty. Fashionable clothes and makeup hardly exist. Most clothing comes in harsh fabrics, dreary colours and unfashionable styles.

Taking pictures is only allowed if you are far away from places related to state security, like industry and the military. You are constantly being watched. The housekeeper on your hotel floor, the clerks at the reception, the man in a black leather jacket on the corner of the street. There is no freedom of speech.

Yet, if you overlook the negative, the positive appears. Polish women are beautiful and elegant. Even with the absence of fashionable clothes in the stores, many dress with chic. In neat little dresses or suits, with colourful scarves tossed around their necks, they stride the streets with poise and charm. I've been told that many make their own clothes, or have them custom-made. There is a cultural life here, too. Mur and I went to a matinee of *Don Carlos* at the elegant Warsaw opera house. All the costumes were made out of black fabric. It was interesting and dramatic, though quite sombre.

Yesterday, I bought a newspaper and eight cakes, and went to Park Ujazdowski to sit down next to a pond of swans. I covered the pigeon-poo-coated bench with the newspaper, then feasted on the cakes. Oh, those cakes! The ones from the Café Ziemianski are particularly beguiling to the eye and titillating to the palate. In the warmth of the Polish sun, I savoured the apple Charlotte, the chocolate-filled Dobos cake, and the little vanilla-cream babas whose custard contains not only a divinity of taste, but also a happy memory from before the war.

Tadeusz comes early in the morning and we make plans on how to search for Basia. Mur stays behind at the University of Warsaw. It's just Tadeusz and I. I feel uneasy about being alone with him. The memory of our near-intimacy lingers, and, what's worse, we have grown quite far apart now.

But I am anxious to solve the mystery surrounding my sister.

All the necessary addresses are in the red file. Also the black and white photos of Basia, particularly one, larger than the rest. That's the picture in which my sister is sitting on the grass with two other children. Yet I hadn't noticed before how frightened were the eyes of these children, and how skeptical—if one can describe this as a little girl's facial expression—is the look on Basia's face. Her shapely mouth is frozen in a grimace. A long shadow falls across the grass over the children, framing them in a darkness separate from the sunlight which brightens the surrounding bushes. Who or what were the children looking at? Perhaps the person taking the photo frightened them. Could that someone have been Roman Mortynski?

We ride in Tad's borrowed car out to Kolkov, where Mortynski lives. Tad says it's only about a forty-five minute drive from Warsaw.

It's a warm day. The Polish countryside glistens in the sun. The fields are green with corn and gold with wheat. Forests of pine, birch, and oak emerge. Scattered here and there are farmlands studded by fruit trees, and decorating the roadside are bluebells, daisies, and poppies.

Air seems not to flow, or am I simply afraid to breathe for fear of disturbing it, as in the war days when I was fearful that someone might hear me and inform on me.

We enter the village of Kolkov. It hasn't changed. The

houses are of wood or stucco. The roads dusty. Not a soul to be seen. But, like the rest of the countryside, it is peaceful.

"It's my village. Remember?" announces Tad proudly. "We're approaching the street where the Mortynskis live."

At the sound of that name, fear destroys my feeling of tranquillity, but that man has to be faced sooner or later.

We stop at a fenced-off property. The house, built of wood, is set deeply in a treed garden. We get out of the car and walk in through the black iron gate. An angry growl stops us in our tracks. Then another and another. Something is moving among the trees, rushing toward us.

Suddenly, two huge black dogs with fang-like teeth spring from the bushes and jump into our faces, yelping like frenzied demons. I am petrified, but Tad motions me to stand still. They must be police dogs. Tad begins to wrestle with the one that had caught his sleeve. The other is growling at me, baring those awful teeth. When he is about to grab my arm, I begin to scream.

"Help! Help!" I yell. Tad is on the ground, fighting the other dog. There is blood on his arm.

"Rex, Rollo!" shouts a man's voice. "Sit!" In a moment, the two monster dogs turn into mice and, with their tails down, scoot back into their respective doghouses, inconspicuously hidden among the bushes close to the house.

A stout middle-aged man comes down a path toward us. I instantly recognize him as Roman Mortynski, my father's one-time best friend.

He studies us intently, then lowers his eyes for a moment. In that instant I know he has also recognized me.

"Slava Lenska?" he says slowly, in a quiet yet deadly sounding tone of voice.

I nod and quietly introduce Tad, whose bloodied arm hangs from his torn shirt.

"I am sorry about this," he says, looking at Tad's arm. "I will find a bandage for you. Come in," he offers in the same deadly tone.

We follow him into the house.

"My wife is not home today. She is working," Mortynski says briefly. "Please sit down," he adds, pointing to the chairs at the table.

I glance around quickly. So this was where little Basia once lived, or still lives, for all I know.

The main room has a dining table in the centre and couches on the sides. The furniture is of light-coloured wood, and the couches are strewn with cushions. There are books on the table. I notice several novels for young girls, including *The Princess Dzavaha*, my favourite, and *W Swiecie Dziewczat—In The World of Young Girls*. Who can be reading books like these, here?

"Do you have children?" I ask with difficulty.

Mortynski shrugs his shoulders and shakes his head. "You know, I am sure," he speaks pointedly, "that my former wife Anna and I are childless."

He sweeps the books off to the side of the table and places a fruit bowl filled with red apples in front of us. A juicy decoy. They do look succulent.

"They're from our own garden," he says invitingly,

following my gaze. Sure. Although I am eighteen years old, I am still influenced by Grimm's fairy tales. I can't help comparing Mortynski's dark looks with those of the witch who had poisoned the red apple before offering it to Snow White. We all know she wanted her dead.

Dead! I think back to Papa's file. Mortynski wanted him dead, and now it's me. In these surroundings, my mind conjures up the grotesque in every scene.

Mortynski brings a cloth for Tad's arm, and a bandage. I bathe Tad's wound and wrap the bandage around his arm. With his free hand Tad helps himself to an apple. I don't dare eat anything in the house of a man who did to us what Mortynski has done. I feel as if Papa were watching my every move as I sit in the house of this traitor.

My leg strikes something under the table. A growl. I jump up. "How did these dogs get back in the house?"

"They have their own entrance. Don't worry," says Mortynski coyly, "it's only Rex and Rollo." There is a warning in his voice: One wrong move, and you get it. These are obviously the dogs Papa had once told me about, Mortynski's police dogs. When the Nazis fled he took several of their killer dogs into his home. Could these be still the same dogs?

After all, when it all happened, only nine years ago, they may have been pups.

"May I look around?" I ask.

"Please yourself," says the man sarcastically. "Afterwards, you can tell me why you're here."

I go into the kitchen. On a table in the corner propped up against the wall stands an open student's briefcase.

There are school paints inside, and a white hair ribbon. Strange. If they don't have children, what are all these juvenile things doing here?

I follow a small corridor and try to open one of the doors. It's locked. I try another and this one is locked too. There is only one more left. The bathroom.

There is nothing much here, except a jar of powder and a bottle of cologne. There are no cupboards or drawers to open.

I return. Mortynski and Tad are engaged in conversation. The word "Party" is mentioned. Tad's ID card is on the table.

"Your friend here is also a Party member," says Mortynski, his arm sweeping the air toward Tad with feigned respect. Though he speaks articulately, the sound of his voice has changed. It is now high pitched, oozing with respect, a falsetto.

"...and in quite a high position I might say," he says, his eyes fixed hawkishly on me. "Why, I remember him as just a kid playing on the street."

The situation is becoming ominous. Questions flood my mind. I must, in spite of the dread I feel toward Mortynski, ask him these questions. I am bad at asking questions, prying. But I have to, for Papa's and my sister's sake.

"Whose is this teenage book, and student's briefcase?" I force myself to speak.

"We have my brother's daughter staying with us," he replies quickly.

"Where is she now?" helps Tad.

"She is out with a friend."

"What happened to Basia?" I press on, desperately trying to sound cool. I take out my sister's photograph and place it on the table.

Mortynski looks at it, then lowers his eyes.

"You must tell us. We'll pay you for the information." I dare farther out into the quicksand, knowing how money hungry he was during the war.

Mortynski's eyes light up at the sound of the word "pay." "Well, it was like this. When the Gestapo came, my wife and the child went with them. I stayed at home."

"What happened afterwards?"

"I..." he hesitates then goes on. "I tried to find her."

"And did you?" I hold my breath.

Mortynski's fingers begin to thump the table. "Ask Anna. I told you the Gestapo came and took her away with your sister, then Anna came back alone.

"As a matter of fact, Anna doesn't live with me anymore. She is in Warsaw. Go and see her there." He scribbles an address on a piece of paper.

"Now just a minute here," intervenes Tad. "You must know what happened."

"Only vaguely," replies Mortynski carefully. He is probably beginning to be wary of Tad. "Anna and I broke up shortly after the Gestapo took Basia. She wouldn't talk to me, and then she left. I haven't seen her for years."

"But there is women's cologne and face powder in the washroom," I dare again.

"They belong to my brother's daughter, my thirteen-year-old niece.

Ridiculous. A thirteen-year-old girl in Poland would not be allowed to use such sophisticated cosmetics. Even in Canada it would be iffy. I feel drained and want to get out of there. I sense Mortynski's cruelty, and a panicky feeling comes over me. My body pulsates in the frenzied rhythm of a beaten drum.

I tell Tad I want to leave. He gets up reluctantly, throwing me a peculiar look. One of the dogs crawls out from under the table and bares his teeth again; the other dog does the same at the door.

Mortynski again silences them with one word. "Sit!"

We are halfway to the iron gate when he begins to shout like a crazed man.

"And don't come snooping around here any more! Your father owes me, do you understand? He owes me!" he yells, waving his fist in the air.

A red cloud of anger closes in on me. I hurl around and yell back.

"My father is dead. You wanted him dead, didn't you, didn't you?" I shout. I should have added, "and you, a blackmailer, you are the one who should die."

The door to the house slams shut. Mortynski disappears. The two hostile dogs on the steps growl.

I nudge Tad to get out of here pronto.

"He's a liar," says Tad, speeding toward Zalesie, where I had lived with Babushka during the war.

"We shouldn't have left so quickly." He goes on, "You could have asked him more questions. He was lying and putting you on. I was going to straighten that out but you decided to leave. I've never thought of you as a coward.

What are you so afraid of when you have me to protect you?"

That hurt! I am not a coward. I am tired. Although he set out to help me, he doesn't understand that I don't trust him completely. It's hard to understand people like us, the survivors, emotionally maimed by war. War alters people. Immigration alters people. Daily association with certain objects, persons, and events brings back our fears. Like mine.

Even now, when I hear an ambulance, it screams inside my head like an air raid siren. When I hear thunder, it explodes in my head like a bomb. When I enter a bakery and smell bread, a gnawing grows in my stomach like hunger. I want to take all the bread home, remembering that during the war we never had enough.

We pass by what seem like deserted villages. They haven't changed since 1943. The people living in them are hidden from the main road by fruit trees and fences with birds perching on top.

The forests and the barns are the same ones that housed Jews on the run to safety. Some were chased away by the owners, others given a chunk of bread then chased like unwanted pests. Persecution was their shell shock. Hiding was their dangerous game with death. Lying about their identity was their ticket to survival. There were many like me. Children who at the age of eight were forced into adulthood. These children had lost their childhood. Yet many survived, while others, a million and a half of them, were brutally murdered. My sister may have been one of them. Why had I survived? This nagging thought has never left me, but kept my spirit wandering in the desert like a punishment.

Why doesn't anyone understand?

"I couldn't stand being with Mortynski in the same room," I finally try to explain. "I couldn't cope. The man is evil. Besides, we're not through with him yet."

"Nor he with us," remarks Tad.

He pulls over to the side of the road and takes a bag from the back seat. Inside are a flask and two sandwiches. He offers me a cheese sandwich and a sip of wine from the flask. I drink it reluctantly, but the wine is warm and soothing.

I calm down and change the subject.

"Why are you so important?" I ask, though I know.

"I can't tell you specifically. We don't discuss these things with outsiders."

So that's what he thinks of me.

"Mur undoubtedly told you that I am in charge of censorship."

"Explain!"

"We don't have freedom of speech or the press here. Everything that is publicly disseminated has to fit the ideology; it has to serve the common good of all our people. Individual rights are not recognized here, as they are by the laws of the Western World. What is good for the people here is decided by the State, not by a few individuals."

"So it's all just propaganda!" I cry outraged. "Just like the rot Nazis tried to feed to Europeans about the Jews!"

Tad looks around uncomfortably. "It's a good thing no one heard you," he says stiffly. "I know the difference between lies and truth. But my job is what it is."

"You're like the police. And a hypocrite." I said contemptuously. "How can you write poetry as well?"

"I am the police," he replies grimly.

I can't believe I am here with a policeman!

"And why can't I write?" Tad goes on. "Mao Tse-Tung—the Chinese leader—has written poetry."

"I know who Mao Tse-Tung is. Our newspapers describe him as the dictator of China."

I am constantly amazed at how much Tad knows of the world. He doesn't seem to be full of propaganda himself, although he censors the truth coming from the West, deciding what news the Poles will be allowed to read. My father believed in freedom, tolerance and creativity. He practised all of the things he preached, except when I became interested in makeup and boyfriends. Then he became intolerant and dictatorial. I could never understand his contradictory nature.

And here is the controversial Tad. What attracts me to him is this curious combination of policeman and poet. No matter how he explains what he does, I still don't understand him. Men are so puzzling!

À Déjà Vu

We ride in silence.

"Where are we going?" I ask Tad. The Mortynski visit has had a sobering effect on both of us.

"It's a surprise."

"I thought we are going to Zalesie." I can't imagine what could be surprising around these parts.

We pass by a sign that says "Malinow." It's not far from Kolkov.

"This is where my grandfather's Rose Villa is!"

Tad sports a little smile at the corners of his mouth. "We're going to Zalesie afterwards. I read about the villa in your file. I looked it up in the county registry, and voilà! Your grandfather is registered there as the owner."

I groan with disbelief. Tad is not as fed up with the whole thing as I thought he'd be by now.

We're on a road called "Flower Avenue."

Tad stops the car next to a wire fence around a property with a pine forest, bush, a garden, and four houses.

We get out of the car and walk gingerly toward the property. There is the house I remember, in tan wood with heart-shaped cut-outs around the windows. It's the house where we used to spend our summer vacations. Here are my young roots, in this corner where the sunflowers still grow taller than I was then. I gaze into their round faces and see a bee sucking gold blood from silken petals.

Here, I wandered through the forest as a child and ate black bread hot from the oven, made by the peasants living and working on the property.

Here, I first encountered the sunflower garden growing not far from the house, in a garden like this one.

Here, I first imprisoned then released butterflies.

Here, I waged war on the bees after one got caught in my hair and bit me on the head, where I still have a red mark.

Here, I had tapeworms and sleepwalked.

Here, Papa argued with Grandfather about escaping the imminent German invasion of Poland. No sooner had Grandfather said no than German planes bombed the bank where he kept all of his wealth.

Here I first experienced an air raid, fear, and the death of a baby in a pink bonnet, killed by a bullet from a low-flying German plane.

Here is where I lost my childhood.

Two women, an old man, and a young boy file out of my grandfather's house. They look shabby but clean. They must be poor folk. No poorer, though, than we immigrants were when we went to Canada, having lost everything here.

"What d'you folks want?" asks the old man, staring at us as if he were seeing ghosts.

"We want to know who this property belongs to," says Tad politely.

"Nobody now. The state rented it out to us in 1949," says the older woman. "This property once belonged to a wealthy Jewish family, but they deserted it."

Yes, I want to shout, and now you're looking at the owner! But Tad's warning glance stops me.

"It never belonged to anybody before," yells the old man at the old woman. "It was just a heap of old deserted buildings."

"We've had to work hard to keep this going," says the younger, hard-looking woman with a cigarette in her mouth. The young boy picks up a stick off the ground and points it at us. "You get out of here or I'll clobber both of you." He raises the stick and starts after us. Tadeusz walks over to him and yanks the stick out of hand, then tosses it far away. The boy hurls himself at Tad. Tad turns him around and kicks his backside as if it was a soccer ball. The boy cries out in pain and rolls down a small hill, his face covered in dirt.

"And don't come snooping here again or I'll report you!" yells the old man.

Tad takes my arm and we leave. We get into the car. They follow us just enough to have a peek at us leaving.

I leave this place with ugly feelings.

There is nothing left to love here except a childhood memory and the language in which I learned to define my first perceptions of beauty in nature—its textures, tastes, smells—and a deadly fear about the world. A child's language without words that described my life.

From somewhere in my mind I gather enough strength to promise myself that one day I will return. That I will take back what is rightfully mine.

We go on to Zalesie, the village in which I hid from the Nazis under an assumed identity. It's only half an hour's drive from Malinow. We look for Honey Street no. 25.

As we round the corner I immediately see my beloved grandmother's place. Its grey brick chimney peeks out of the trees, followed by a black, sloping rooftop on a square, white stucco house, surrounded by a garden and tall trees. It's like a dove nestling among green giants. In contrast to Mortynski's evil house, I view this as a place where goodness and peace, respect for nature and human life ruled supreme. On seeing it now for the first time since the war, I realize that it wasn't only Papa who saved my life, but also his mother, my babushka.

I try hard not to cry in front of Tadeusz, lest I appear a wimp.

In the garden, across the road from Babushka's house, a woman with one arm is raking leaves. Her other arm is an empty sleeve folded and tucked into the blouse's hollow armpit. Her face is wrinkled like the skin of an old potato, and she wears a Dutch-style hat over greying locks. She resembles an elf in a brown dress.

We get out of the car. The woman turns her head away

from her chores and slowly walks up to the fence. She scans our faces inquisitively. Her gaze rests on my face, but her eyes seem to be staring inward, perhaps into the past.

"Could you by any chance be little Irenka?" she asks softly. She remembers the child from across the road, hiding under a false name.

"You must be Zofia," I say excitedly.

"Yes, yes, come in, come in," she urges, opening the gate with her one arm.

Tadeusz looks at us both, astonished. On the way to the house I briefly explain this part of my past.

"Sit down, sit down. I will make you some tea." Zofia disappears into a kitchen to the right of the front entrance, just as I remember it from 1943.

Nothing has changed here, I observe, looking around the dark room. The same old dampness, armchairs smelling of mouldy fabric. The very same bookshelves filled with volumes that saved my sanity during my incarceration in this village. They taught me the value of reading. Here I learned the magic of transcending the fear and longing for my family by entering the world of characters who also struggled for survival.

I can still see, as I did then, the tracks of mouse feces lining the wooden floor between the dining area and the kitchen. I can still hear, as in those days, the scraping and squeaking of rats and their snaking shapes outlined in the frosted glass door that separated me and the bookshelves from the pantry. A big black cat would spring from nowhere and land on the floor with a thud, and start scratching the door of the pantry with his sharp claws. Then, mercifully, Zofia would open the pantry door and let the fat cat chase his prey. Sensing my fear, she would snuggle me close to her dirty apron that smelled of carrots and onions. She would pacify me with a shrivelled apple from her winter store in the cellar, and speed me back home, across the street, my beloved books tied up in a tea towel.

A cat crawls stealthily by. He is black, fat, and old. Can it be the same one I feared then? Impossible. Cats don't live that long. Is all this possible and real, I wonder? Is it all a déjà vu?

"Zofia was very good to me during the war," I whisper to Tad, who is seated next to me, silently surveying the room. He nods approvingly.

Zofia returns with tea in glasses in silver holders.

"Your grandmother gave me those," she says proudly. "She told me that they were a part of her wedding trousseau from Russia. Both the sterling silver holders and the crystal glasses." She reminisces, fingering a glass with her one hand.

She offers us raspberry liquor. "Made it myself," she says proudly, pouring the pinky-white liquid into tiny crystal glasses.

"I loved that lady, your babushka," she goes on. "Never knew she was Jewish till after the war. It wouldn't have mattered anyway. I hid a Jewish man up in my attic, and no one ever knew. My husband and I shook from fear when the Nazi soldiers came to inquire about the death of the Volksdeutscher and his wife. Irka's parents, remember, Irenka? Of course I know your real name is Slava. Your grandma told me. She died of a broken heart. Her beloved son, your father, and you left for America, and her other son murdered in Treblinka. She also had a young daughter who died from pneumonia before the war." Zofia paused for a moment, brushing off a tear with an earth-blackened finger. "She said that you looked like that daughter.

"She was a good neighbour. Always there when needed. Vlad, who was her Christian husband only during the war, promised to help her through in exchange for her house. He was a penniless drunk from Lodz. Even during the war when you were still here, remember? He'd get picked up in the ditch by the locals every other day, and she'd have to undress him and put him to bed. He was a heavy man. Made her life a nightmare, beat her, too.

"One morning, after you left for Canada, she knocked on my door, white as a ghost, with bruises under her eyes, holding her chest. She gave me a bundle and said to give it to you if you ever came back. That night, she passed away."

I listen with horror. How could Papa have left Babushka with this man who beat her up? And yet the same man helped save our lives. How can good and evil twist together into such a formidable knot?

Zofia shuffles back into the kitchen, and soon appears with a small parcel wrapped in cloth. Through the tissue, I instantly recognize Babushka's embroidered tablecloth. It has sunflowers and green leaves all over it.

I quickly unwrap it. Inside the cloth is a small grey felt bag, a book, and a letter. The book is familiar. It is the 1935 edition of a collection of works by the brilliant Russian writer, Alexander Pushkin. On the long winter nights of 1943, I can still hear Babushka's voice reading his great epic poem "The Gypsies" to me. Between the book's pages lies a photograph of a young girl with long hair and a beautiful face. Pressed between the pages are also dried pink flowers and several stalks of wheat, among the poems written in the Cyrillic alphabet.

The grey felt bag contains a thick gold chain and a gold hexagonal pendant, studded with yellow stones, ambers I think. I open the letter, and read, translating into English as has become my habit.

My Darling Slava,

I am old, weak, and tired. I hope that one day you will return, and I have instructed Zofia to make sure you get these things: The cloth, the gold pendant that belonged to your aunt Luda from St. Petersburg, and the book. I cannot send these things to you because of the censorship at customs, so I am leaving them in Zofia's safekeeping. She is a good woman.

How I miss you all. I am left alone here with thoughts and memories of you and, though I am lonely, my heart is filled with love. The memories are painful, too, as is solitude. I fear that I shall soon die. Life has exhausted me and I welcome the peace death promises. These are the things I want you to have, as I know your soul, and that it will receive accordingly these few offerings. Everything else is gone.

Whatever you do, Slavenka, watch out for M. He stole almost everything from us.

> Your loving babushka forever
> *Katya Lenska*
> Zalesie, February 21, 1949

The writing ends with a line zigzagging across the page, as if the pen had run out of ink together with my babushka's life.

She died only a few days after Papa.

Unable to speak, I hand the letter to Tad and hang the gold disk around my neck. Filled with remorse and feelings of loss, I excuse myself and run onto the road and across the street.

I ring the bell on the gate of my grandmother's house. After what seems like a long while, a woman comes out and stands in front of the garden gate, barring entry. She appears sour and pale. Her hair is pulled back into a severe knot, and her dress is soiled.

"What do you want?" she asks sullenly.

"I want to see the house. I used to live here."

The woman regards me suspiciously, her eyelids fluttering like nervous moths.

"You don't want to remember all that again. What for? Besides it is not your house any longer."

She locks the gate and turns away.

My feet won't move. Though the key to this place is lost forever, I am captivated by the scent of flowers wafting from the garden that used to be Babushka's; the scent of her simple freshly-baked butter cake; of fried onions and boiled potatoes. I can almost feel the ache of hunger in my stomach, remembering when we didn't have enough to eat.

Slowly I walk away and around to the back of the garden, examining the familiar trees and bushes through the fence. The smelly outhouse is still there next to the hole, my hideaway for three nights and days when the Nazis came to the village to search all the homes for Jews in hiding and partisans who prowled the forest.

There are still the raspberry bushes growing here. It was among those bushes that, one night, Vlad and Babushka buried the treasure.

I can almost see them as then, when I watched through the window of that house, straining my eyes in the twilight. They were bending over the earth they were about to dig up. Babushka held a box filled with pearls, solid gold trinkets, diamond bracelets, pendants and other precious jewels. Vlad holding a spade. Babushka bustliing around pretending that she was picking raspberries.

They buried the box deep in the ground, and covered it with earth. They marked the spot by planting an apple tree nearby. The apple tree is still growing. What about the treasure? Undoubtedly Vlad dug it out and took it back to Lodz with him. That's where he came from and that's where, we heard, he returned to die some years after the war.

Loneliness engulfs me such as I have often felt throughout my post-war life. Or is it aloneness?

I walk back to Zofia's to say goodbye and tell her that I may not come this way again. She hugs me affectionately. Once more I inhale her well-remembered scent of tea, lemon, garlic, and garden vegetables.

Tad is silent. In his silence, I intuit much contemplation on all that is happening around him. Perhaps his own memories are surfacing. Perhaps he too is remembering his childhood in a Polish village.

We leave Honey Street, my mind still clinging to those memories with the desperation of someone who clutches at seaweed for survival. I am still linked to those times. Though they are filled with horror, they make up my past, my history and roots. They are all I have left of a stolen childhood. These memories are so real to me now that the present seems only a silly grey mouse running through a maze, backwards.

10
The Inquiry

The next day, back in Warsaw, Mur offers to come with me to see Anna Mortynski.

On the way, we pass the monument to the Warsaw ghetto martyrs. He asks me if I know anything about the Jewish Resistance of 1943.

"They were real heroes," I explain. "While Jews were being deported to the concentration camps, and the Nazis were about to liquidate the ghetto, they held off the German army for about three weeks. Imagine!" I tell him.

"I still remember the red sky and the black smoke over Warsaw the day the Nazis burned the ghetto. It looked as if a volcano had exploded, spilling molten lava into the sky. My grandmother squeezed my hand so hard it hurt, while the peasants stood around grinning and joking. Later, inside the house, Babushka whispered to me that the Warsaw ghetto fighters had saved the honour and the pride of the Jewish people.

Mur is silent. He looks around the barren field that

was once the ghetto.

"I can say I am ashamed of our people's indifference," he says. "When I joined the partisan army I tried my best to purge myself of the guilt. I shot a Volksdeutscher in one of the villages. We knew that he had informed on Jews in hiding."

"What village was that?" I asked, wondering if it was the same village I was in.

"It was in Upper Zalesie."

Fate has its gypsy ways. I tell Mur about Irka, the little girl whose father was a Volksdeutscher, a Pole of German origin, who informed on Jews and partisans. I had unwittingly befriended her in a wheat field in Upper Zalesie while hiding with Babushka and Vlad, and had even accepted her invitation to tea.

"Didn't you know who her father was when you went there? He was one of the most dangerous Nazis, a member of the Gestapo planted in that village. He was a Jew hunter. We hunted many like him in the adjoining villages. Kolkov, for example. You were lucky."

Mur sounds somewhat distraught. I guess the war got to him too.

"I know. I mostly survived by pure, inexplicable luck. Kolkov was where my sister may have been murdered," I tell him. My heart is beating as if it has three fists pounding my rib cage.

I tell him more about Mortynski and his wife, and how he behaved when Tad and I went to inquire about Basia.

"My guess is that he was an informer, too."

"But surely he wouldn't have informed on Basia, at a

danger to himself? Anyone hiding a Jew was automatically sentenced to death."

"As a Nazi sympathizer, Mortynski might have used his connections to save your sister. Or perhaps he informed on her instead, in order to destroy your father."

How can one fathom such unspeakable cruelty? There was no language in which to understand it.

I tell Mur about how guilty I still feel to have survived instead of my sister.

"Let me get this straight. You were supposed to stay with Mortynski, and your sister was to go to Babushka. But things changed when you got ill, and the plan was reversed. Why?"

"Because Papa had arranged that on a specific day, someone would take one of us to a designated place. The first place was Mortynski's villa, on the day that I got ill. So my sister went instead of me."

Mur is silent again. We stand mute, like two statues, in the ashen desert of the burned ghetto.

"You should write a story about all this," he speaks at last.

He sounds like Joshua.

"I have," I reply. "But people don't seem to want to hear about it."

We start to walk again.

"Do you know why that is?" says Mur pensively. "Because people can't face what they don't understand. And they don't understand the meaning of this genocide and its lasting effect on our society. They can't grasp the existence of barbarism in a civilized country like Germany. It poses questions about themselves, their racist views and prejudices."

His words astonish me. I wish that someday I will be able to articulate my thoughts as powerfully. When he speaks like a philosopher and poet, Mur sounds like Papa.

We arrive at Anna Mortynski's apartment building. It is a sterile, post-war structure, lacking artistic design. It stands on the edge of the ghetto next to a gang of six or seven others just like it. They are all square, grey, gargantuan boxes, without flowers or trees gracing the ground around them. They stand on the ashes of the dead and on the edge of children's nightmares.

We enter the building, walk up several flights of stairs, down a long dim corridor of countless brown doors, and knock on door number 29.

After three or four knocks, a woman opens it, holding the knob with misshapen arthritic fingers.

"I knew you would come. Roman telephoned me that you were in Warsaw. Slava, please come in," she says, smiling at Mur. She has a pleasant though aged face. I remember her as a pretty woman with sparkling brown eyes and lustrous chestnut hair. She seemed sad even in those days, before the war, in their lovely villa, when she was telling Mama that she and Roman couldn't have children. My parents and the Mortynskis were the best of friends then. Of course this was why my father turned to them for help when the Nazis were planning to gather all the children in the ghetto and send them to the concentration camp.

To think of that friendship now!

She shows us into a minuscule sitting room containing three chairs and a table.

"I don't have much space here," she apologizes. "Just a tiny one bedroom, and I am lucky to have even that. Last year, when Roman found out I had rheumatism, he threw me out of the house and took himself a mistress." Anna begins to cry. "Slava, you remember our beautiful villa, don't you? Now Roman is great friends with the Communists. He made some deal with them and they let him keep the house. You know Roman, he always goes with the winning side." She is silent for a moment. "Let me bring you something cold to drink," she says, wiping the perspiration off her forehead.

"Now we know for sure that Mortynski is a liar," I tell Mur. "He told us a different story. He said that his wife left him."

The last time I saw Anna was in 1939, just before the Blitzkrieg. There were parties in her home then, drink and good food. I remember her pantry full of fruit preserves. She gave me chocolate. She appeared kind.

Now, thirteen years later, Anna looks old and unhappy.

"This is quite the story unfolding here," says Mur, while we wait for Anna to return.

"Why do you think that?" I ask, intrigued. It's hard to think clearly. All I can think of now is Basia.

"Look around you," says Mur. "Just like you described it at Mortynski's house. A shelf of books for young people, a folded cot by the wall. And Mortynski, first a Nazi collaborator, then a Commie party member.

"But let's wait and see what this lady has to say," he adds.

Anna returns with a tray of cookies and juice.

"Here," she says, putting down the tray and handing me a photograph, "this is the last picture I took of Basia. A few days before Roman and the Gestapo took her away from me."

My little sister is sitting on a log holding a ball in her plump baby hands. The black and white landscape suggests that it was a cloudy day. She seems older, about five in this picture, unlike the other where she was only three years old. We had been told that she died when she was four.

"Where was this photo taken?" I ask.

Anna opens her mouth to speak but says nothing.

I look at Mur. He stirs uncomfortably in his chair, as if to say, "let's get on with it."

"I think you should tell Slava all there is to know, Mrs. Mortynska," says Mur finally, in his strong, self-assured voice. "She came all this way, in spite of many difficulties, to find out about her sister."

Anna's face softens somewhat. "Oh, I've cried so many tears over this child, I became dry." She is knotting the corner of a napkin with nervous hands. "I loved her too, you know. The fact is that one day, unexpectedly, the Gestapo came for her and took her away. Someone had informed on her. She and my husband: they left together with the Gestapo. I never saw her after that. Roman returned alone. You'd better forget about Basia," she says, looking at me intently. Her voice becomes harsh suddenly. "Forget her. Do you understand?"

"What are these books and dolls doing here?" I manage to sound firm.

"They belong to a little girl I babysit for a friend...uhh...her name is Tereska, she is my friend," she offers uncertainly.

A dead-end answer.

Mur's forehead creases with puzzlement, and his eyes begin to blink erratically. This often happens, I've noticed, when he is angry. He is also shaking his head from side to side, as if to say something is wrong here. Silently, I agree with him. What Anna has told us we already knew. Except for one thing: Roman said that Anna was the one who left the villa with the child and the Gestapo. Anna has just told us the opposite.

We have conflicting stories from the only two people who really know what happened to my sister.

"I have to go out now," says Anna in that same sharp tone of voice. "I am sorry. I can't help you any more."

We get up to leave.

Mur stops at the threshold. "Why does your story differ from your husband's?" he asks, explaining Mortynski's version.

Why didn't I ask that question?

Anna flinches slightly. "You can't believe Roman. He doesn't understand the meaning of truth. Goodbye." She begins to close the door, forcing us to back out.

"They're both hiding something," says Mur, outside. "The old man is hungry for money, and the old lady wants to keep things as they are, however that is. I am only speculating, but it seems likely that Anna was or is more attached to your sister than her husband. Roman will sell anything and anyone. Maybe he did save your sister by bribing the Nazis."

All these possibilities, while they are bizarre, excite me. We must be onto something, and that means I must probe further.

"Do you know anyone else who might offer the truth?" queries Mur.

Do I? "Maybe Zofia in Zalesie knows more than she let on. If Babushka confided in her then maybe she told her something about this."

Back at the hotel, there is a message from Tad, saying he will be joining us for lunch.

We meet in our hotel's outdoor cafe. It is a gorgeous summer day. Tad and Mur are discussing Mur's reading at the University of Warsaw. I realize that these two have other pots on the stove, while I have only one: my sister. What happened to her?

Eventually the conversation turns to Basia, and Mur describes this morning's events to Tadeusz.

At the end of our conversation, I decide that Zofia definitely knows more than she has let on. Tad and Mur agree enthusiastically. Before long, we are on our way back to Zalesie, and Honey Street.

"By the way," says Mur, "have you noticed that we have been followed ever since we left Warsaw?"

I turn around. There is a black car riding at a careful distance behind us.

11

The Truth?

There are too many loose strands in my sister's story. I grope for truth like a blind person trying to thread a needle. Everywhere I look, I see only fragments.

Tad, Mur, and I arrive at Zofia's garden gate.

The black car behind us stops much farther down the road.

Zofia is in the same place she was the last time we came, tending to her garden, weeding a flowerbed with her one arm.

She looks up from under the triangular corner of her Dutch hat. Dragging her long, dirty-white apron on the ground, she moves closer to the gate.

"Oh, it's you," she says with a smile of recognition. "Come in." The gate swings open and we are invited inside.

She immediately brings us three glasses of lemonade, which we drink thirstily. Then I explain the purpose of our visit, but say nothing about being followed.

In a feverish spew of sentences, I tell her the whole story.

Zofia's calm demeanour doesn't change, but her eyes become wider and wider. After I finish she crosses herself, reciting a prayer to Virgin Mary.

Zofia seems moved beyond ordinary speech.

After a moment's silence she returns to us from her prayer.

"I heard a strange story about something that took place in 1943, the same time that all those horrible things were happening...that you told me about..." Zofia pauses to cough as if she were choking on her own words. I sit on edge, and my two friends stare at the old woman as if she were a magician.

"It was known that a prominent Pole in Kolkov," continues Zofia, "with a strong connection to a Nazi Commandant offered the Gestapo a bribe of jewellery for not killing a Jewish child, a little girl of four or five. The Commandant promised to wait for the bribe to be paid and in the meantime placed the child in a nearby convent. The Pole then went to an old woman, the girl's grandmother, and blackmailed her for her possessions. It is said that she gave him some jewels."

Zofia comes closer and begins to whisper. "I saw Mortynski come to your grandmother's house the night after she died and dig up a box from the corner of the garden. I didn't know whose it was, so decided to mind my own business. Everyone was afraid of Mortynski, including me, and I thought he might have seen me spying on him.

"That's all I know," she concludes sadly. "I was never certain, Slava, if that child was your sister. Your grandmother never talked about her. But I know she hated Roman Mortynski."

How to weed out speculation and lies? There has to be a way.

Andrzej and Tad are with me all the way.

Zofia agrees to help.

"You know," she says, "a caretaker couple who worked at the Mortynski villa used to bring messages to your grandmother from the master himself. Although they were undoubtedly sworn to secrecy, they are very old now. Mortynski keeps them poor as church mice. Money may speak. American dollars or British pounds are worth gold around here."

I tell her that we are willing to pay these people, if they are willing to talk. I feel like a detective in an American movie.

Zofia makes a phone call. In the meantime Tad and Mur are deep in discussion about the dangers of all this snooping. What if the Party authorities get onto us? And heaven help us if Mortynski is one of them. Although Tad is an important party member, and a member of the secret police, there are always higher-ups who wield more power. And how are we going to ditch the black car on our tail?

"Don't worry so much," says Tad. "In this system, everyone is responsible for everyone, and everyone in power is answerable to someone else. In the end nobody knows who is the highest."

Mur laughs, then becomes serious. "The authorities probably don't dwell on what the Nazis did. But they don't like foreigners snooping around the country." "Even though you are one of them, you are still helping us," Mur says to Tad.

Tad looks sceptical. "Sure, the Communists may not be upset about what the Nazis did to the Jews, but they hate them for what they did to the Poles during the war. Also to the Russians. Twenty million died."

"I'm afraid for Zofia," I whisper, while she is in the kitchen talking on the phone. Tad falls silent and scratches his head.

"The agents," he says finally, "won't inform the higher ranks about an incident that is so local and personal. They'll probably try to tackle it themselves. We won't fear Mortynski. He is probably aware that we know too much about him: that he was a Nazi collaborator, for example. There. That will work against him. As for the car behind us, I have a plan."

Mur and I admit to being terribly confused, but we are willing to trust Tad.

Zofia returns and tells us that the old janitor couple are at the hospital picking up their medication. She suggests that we all go there. The nurse, who is a good friend of Zofia's, is sympathetic, and promises to hold them till our arrival.

Fate intervenes again.

Zofia asks if she can ride with us. We squeeze into Tad's car, and head for the hospital in Kolkov.

At the entrance to the hospital parking lot we stop in

front of an army jeep with a red cross on it. A hefty woman dressed in a white uniform and a nurse's cap waves to us. The old couple, the caretakers of the Mortynski Villa, are sitting in the jeep. The nurse moves them out to a shady bench in the small garden outside the hospital.

She introduces them as Mr. and Mrs. Kamienny. A bell rings in my head! They are the couple whose peasant hut I used to pass by long ago, on Mortynski's property. They'd invite me in and offer me a fruit drink.

The woman is wearing a heavy wool sweater over a homespun cotton dress, and, on her head, a thick cotton kerchief with red flowers on it. The old man sports a coachman's cap and a well-worn shirt.

The nurse is helpful and interested in our quest. Zofia approaches them. They seem to know her. When she tells them who we are and why we came, the old woman crosses herself, mumbling something.

The old man breaks their silence. He speaks with difficulty. "That evening Gestapo came for little one, Mr. and Mrs. went out with child. Long after they came to villa, alone."

"That's what us know," they say, speaking in the dialect of the country folk.

I offer them ten British pounds but they shake their heads. They don't want it. I tuck it into the woman's sweater pocket.

The meeting is over. Faced with yet a third account of Basia's story I struggle to keep from bursting into tears. The frustration of all this is unbearable.

Suddenly the old woman, who is already back in the jeep, motions me to come over. She stares into me with brown beady eyes, but not unkindly. "I remember you," she says, "you were the older wee one."

She beckons me to come closer. I lean toward her face. "Never tell anyone," she whispers with onion breath, "for he will punish us. We were sworn on Jesus Christ and The Holy Mother. But he no good. Now he play other side. Took from us little scrap of land we had."

Whenever she pauses, I stop breathing. There has to be more. No peasant in the village was ignorant about other folks' business. The white cotton curtains of the little huts in which they lived always had an old baba peering through them. Don't stop, I beg her silently. She motions me to come even closer. She whispers in my ear.

"Evening, they did come back alone, without the child. But I heard them in the night. He shouted at her. She loved the other wee one, but he afraid of trouble with Germans. He was going to bribe them with her gold ring. He talked about going to the convent where the wee one was being held for ransom.

"One day, after the war, he came home, holding a box. When he went back into the house, he forgot to close door. I watched him opening box and taking out all kinds of jewels—gold, silver, pearls! She asked where he got it. He laughed and said he got it from wee one's granny, and he'll get more because she owes him."

The woman pauses for a moment as if afraid to carry on. "You try convent," she whispers, so her husband won't hear. "There's one near. You know nothing. Now we go, and remember what you promised."

I hug the woman, my faith in humanity restored. Just before the jeep pulls away, I catch the old man giving his old wife a look of utter contempt.

While we drive her home, Zofia gives us vague directions on how to get to the convent.

For certain, now, we will have to visit this convent. Also for certain, it is this devil Mortynski who stole the jewels from Babushka's garden.

We drop Zofia off, then follow her directions, but are unable to find the convent, so we decide to park the car and walk. Nobody along the road wants to tell us where it is. People stare at us. They lie and say they don't know. Some shrug their shoulders and walk away. Some talk to Tadeusz. I see the curtains being parted in the houses as we walk past them along the dirt road.

Finally we get to the city hall, where Tad makes inquiries and learns that the convent of Holy Mary is on the edge of town, not far from here. Basia in a convent? Still, after all these years? Horrible thoughts come to me. What if she is there and I don't recognize her? What if I do? What if she has no inkling of who she really is?

The Mother Superior

The convent stands silver-grey among the trees, silent and old like they are. It must have seen more then one war. A tall wood fence surrounds the building. We turn the rusted knob but the black iron gate is locked, like the door I often see in one of my recurring dreams. *There is a closed door. I want to enter through it but have no key. I despair at first, then I look in my hand, and there it is, the key, huge and golden. Just as I begin to open the door, the dream fades without an ending.*

There is a piece of wood tacked onto the side of the gate, with a small bell hanging on a string beneath it. Tad rings the bell.

Mur, as if sensing my uneasiness, stands close to me. He always seems to know what I am feeling. Apprehension and hope walk arm in arm along the dark corridor of memory.

A nun in a black habit comes swiftly toward us.

"What are you seeking here?" she asks. She is young

and pretty, with red cheeks and bright eyes.

With the locked gate between us, I tell her the story, trying hard to be brief. I am used to strangers growing impatient while listening to my strange tale.

The nun listens, fingering her rosary. After I've finished, she opens the gate reluctantly.

"I don't know if I can help you," she says. "You will have to speak with the Mother Superior. Please follow me inside to the waiting room. I will announce you. May I know your names?" She speaks quickly and her cheeks are now very red.

We give her our names.

"My name is Sister Ursula," she throws over her shoulder as we follow her in single file. Tad runs ahead, seemingly fascinated with the sister. Once inside, she tells us to wait in a sunny reception room, then rushes out, black gown swinging above her black oxfords.

Tad is grimacing at the cross on the wall. "Religion is a crutch," he comments.

As usual Mur expounds his philosophy, maintaining that religious practices and beliefs are a private matter for the individual's soul, and are incompatible with political censorship and state ideologies.

"Do you believe in God?" I ask him.

"Sometimes," he replies.

Tad changes the subject. Most probably, Mur is being too philosophical for him.

Sister Ursula rushes back in and breathlessly orders us to follow her. By now I have realized that Sister Ursula does things quickly.

We walk down a long corridor with cream stucco walls. We pass by several brown doors behind which we hear muffled voices. One door opens onto a chapel where a few of the sisters are chanting.

"We are a school as well," explains Sister Ursula, so swift on her heels that we can hardly keep up.

"The security people come here once in a while. They inspect, but say nothing. Religion is very strong among the country folk. So they leave us alone."

We walk into a small dark foyer where the sister tells us to sit down and wait. Exhausted, we flop onto a hard wooden bench.

"You'd better give her the photograph," says Mur.

I explain the photograph to Sister Ursula, who now seems more interested in my story. Mutely, she takes the photo and enters another room, closing the door softly behind her.

The grandfather clock ticks away. It's like waiting for surgery. In a while that has stretched into eternity, the door opens. Sister Ursula steps out and says that I am to go in to speak with the Mother Superior, alone. With no small amount of apprehension, I follow her orders.

A very old woman with a stern face, her black-clad torso half-hidden by a huge desk, motions me to sit down.

"Sister Ursula tells me that you are looking for a Jewish child lost during the war, and that the child is your sister, who may be with us."

I nod in silence.

"I was appointed to this convent after the war," she explains. "But I know from the previous Mother Superior that there were Jewish children hidden here. Also there was a ghetto here in Kolkov. Many Jewish children were taken to the edge of the forest and shot." The Mother Superior stops talking and takes in a sharp breath. Perhaps she is deeply moved. Perhaps she understands. Tears well up in my throat and suddenly I am unable to control their flow. It feels almost unbearable to have encountered this kind of empathy.

She stands up with difficulty, as she is old, and, coming around the desk, cradles my head in the crook of her arm. I feel comforted by the soft texture of her habit.

"Cry, my child, cry," she admonishes. "May your tears absolve the evil that was done."

She smells of incense and the musk of unscented soap.

After a few minutes, when I am in control of my emotions, the Mother Superior returns to her chair and resumes her account.

"Many Jewish children were not claimed after the war. Some of the orphans went on to refugee camps, and from there to Palestine or North America. Others remained here. A very few became nuns, or grew up in Catholic households, not knowing that they were originally Jewish. They were too young to remember their real families, and accepted the Catholic faith and the people who had saved their lives and had taken care of them like their parents would have done."

"My sister Basia was four years old when they told us she had been murdered," I interject. The Mother Superior winces at the word "murdered."

"What reason do you have for believing that your

sister is still alive and that we'd know where she might be? We have many thirteen-year-old girls studying with us, even living here, training to become nuns. It is difficult to identify a thirteen-year-old girl from a four-year-old's photograph."

A vision of Basia in a nun's habit flashes before me, as do other bizarre scenes. Like the day Mama and I searched convents and Catholic schools in Warsaw after the war ended. We scanned the faces of hundreds of six-year-olds, searching for Basia's face, that one beloved face. But it was no use. We walked into each institution with hope and walked out with disappointment. We didn't come here. I wonder why?

"Would you like to see our students?" asks the Mother Superior gently.

Hope leaps up like a wild cat.

"Oh yes, yes, Mother Superior, please."

"Come with me."

Walking behind the Mother Superior, I feel all my nerves prickling my body like needles. Am I cheating history? Trying to change its course by turning the pages backwards? I remember how Papa was pulling his hair out of his skull when he found out about Basia's death from Mortynski. I remember Mama's sad and swollen eyes, and myself, kneeling in prayer before God.

We enter a classroom where girls are studying. It is so quiet in here. They are reading, and a nun, presumably their teacher, sits at her desk, looking on.

"Have a look at the girls," says the Mother Superior, "while I speak with Sister Cecilia." The Mother Superior speaks to her in a hushed tone. She speaks for some time, as the story is long. The teacher keeps on nodding.

I scan the room, feeling awkward about standing in front of the class like an impostor. Some girls just look at me, others smile. Still others look me up and down in a mocking fashion. This is how girls behave in an institution. This is how they greet a stranger.

There are about twenty-five girls. All in their early teens. At least that's what the Mother Superior said before we came in. I scan the blondes; the brunettes; the redheads. They are all clean-cut, wearing navy blue dresses with white collars. How can one of them possibly be Basia? The last time I saw her she was two years old, and in the photograph she is four. Children change in that span of time.

Looking at the photograph, then at the girls, alternately, I examine each face, each feature, each pair of eyes, each nose, each lip, each curl, each hand.

There is one girl to whom my eyes return over and over again. Her blond-brown hair is wavy like mine, and her eyes are green. She has delicate fingers like Mama, and Papa's straight nose.

I walk over to the Mother Superior and tell her about this girl.

"Sister Cecilia will check on her. We don't want to upset these girls. Although most of them are orphans, some have parents and homes and just study with us." The Mother Superior's voice, once gentle, now has an edge to it. She speaks with Sister Cecilia again and ushers me out of the room.

"I must talk with the girl first, then with Sister Cecilia. I will bring her to the library after class and you will speak with her there," says the Mother Superior. "Her name is Teresa, and she is an orphan."

"Teresa?" The name buzzes in my head with familiarity. Wasn't that the name of Anna's friend whose child she babysat? This girl is too old to be babysat, surely. I dismiss the idea as a coincidence.

Feeling uncertain about how to handle this alone, I want to consult with my friends in the waiting room. The Mother Superior understands and lets me return to them.

"We have to wait till Teresa's class ends in another twenty minutes. Then you may return to my office," she says, more kindly now.

Tad and Mur looked alarmed, as if they were beholding a ghost.

"What happened to you in there?" inquires Mur. "You look so pale!" exclaims Tad.

I tell them about Teresa.

13
Teresa

The Mother Superior calls me in and bids me to follow her.

I walk behind her on jellied knees. This always happens when I am walking toward the unknown, as I did during the war when I crossed from the ghetto over to the other side, leaving my parents behind. Now I feel both afraid and anxious about finding Basia or not finding her at all.

At the end of the corridor we turn left into a library.

"Sit down, please," says the Mother Superior, motioning me to a chair at one of the tables. "Teresa will be down in a minute. The poor child has been having a difficult time lately. Bad dreams. She feels that something terrible frightened her once when she was a small child, but can't remember what it was. We can't help her, not knowing very much about her, except that she came to us as an orphan."

We sit at a large table in the centre of the room. It is so highly polished I can see the outline of my head in its brown sheen. Time drags as we wait. If only Mama were here to help. But poor Mama doesn't even know *I* am here. At times all this seems as unreal as if it were a dream, or someone else's story.

Footsteps outside. The door opens, and the girl called Teresa enters.

She walks up to the Mother Superior, bows down and kisses her hand. The Mother Superior gently places her hand on the girl's head. "God bless you, my child, you may sit down. This young woman would like to speak with you for a few minutes. Her name is Slava."

The Mother Superior then turns to me. "If you don't mind, I will stay."

I freeze. What can I say or ask? The girl's olive-green eyes are fixed on me like a cat's. Her pearl-white face is calm, though her hands nervously clasp and unclasp a rosary. She wears her tidy navy dress; her honey-brown hair hangs in ringlets, pinned back with a comb.

Can this young, composed, future nun be my lost Jewish sister?

"Teresa is still studying. She will soon be a novice. She is much too young to become a nun," remarks the Mother Superior, as if she were reading my thoughts.

I nod absentmindedly, trying to formulate an appropriate question.

"Do you remember how you became an orphan?" I blurt out finally.

The girl's eyes are no longer fixed on me. There is something distant in them now, as if they were looking for something within another time or space.

An unbearably long moment of silence ensues as I wait for the answer.

"I think I remember a train," the girl speaks slowly as if in a dream. "A woman held me close. It was Mommy...I was hungry and cold..." The girl's voice breaks slightly, then continues. "Mommy gave me to this woman. There was a lot of commotion around. Then the train stopped. Then Mommy went away. The woman took me somewhere. Mommy never came back. I don't remember anything after that. As I grew older, this couple took me to a convent and left me with the sisters. They'd told me that my real parents gave me away." The girl pauses. She is on the verge of tears. "That I must forget my real parents, because they were my parents now."

Teresa wipes her eyes with her hand. "Why are you asking me all this?"

Mother Superior signals me to go on by nodding her head.

"Because I am looking for my lost sister, Basia, who was said to have been killed during the war. We think that she may be still alive. That maybe the couple who took her in to hide her from the Nazis didn't want to give her back to us after the war. How old were you when you first went to a convent?"

"I was six, I think. Then I left there and came to this convent when I was nine, and I've been here ever since."

"What about that couple?" I probe, hardly knowing what to ask next.

Teresa hesitates.

"A man has been coming to visit me."

"Can you tell me more about him?" I ask, feeling guilty for upsetting this poor girl.

"He is my uncle, the only relative I have," she replies with certainty. "He wants me to become a nun," she adds, her eyes lowered, her graceful hands still playing with the rosary.

I sense a strangeness in her behaviour, and fear in her voice at the mention of her uncle. I show her Basia's photograph.

She takes it and studies it, showing a sign of recognition.

"I remember this dress," she says suddenly. "It had red flowers on it."

Hope enters my heart. Though the photograph is black and white, one could see the pattern of dark flowers scattered all over it on a whitish background.

"Just before I went to that first convent, I remember a big garden, a huge black dog and lots of children playing there. There were several girls dressed in the same dresses."

At the mention of the huge black hound, I envision Mortynski and his dogs. Could the dog have been his?

"Can you recognize this girl?" I ask. "She was four or five at the time."

"She seems to be someone familiar," Teresa says, looking as if she were in a trance. "I remember someone taking pictures at a children's gathering, but I never saw the pictures. My uncle said that all my photos got burned in an accident. So I don't have any."

"Do you know the name of that first convent?" I ask,

struggling for more good questions to ask. I feel tired and pressured, painfully aware of the Mother Superior's fixed gaze on me.

"It's almost time for vespers," announces the Mother Superior suddenly. "Teresa must go now. Besides, that first convent burnt down. It no longer exists."

I feel flustered and disappointed. This is not enough information. I need more. I need more time. Why does the Mother Superior have to interfere? Why doesn't she just go away and leave us alone? I look at my watch and see the deadline has arrived. It's four o'clock.

"You may go now, child," says the Mother Superior to Teresa.

The girl hesitates, then bows again to the Mother Superior and, casting an inquisitive glance in my direction, flutters gently out of the room, like a butterfly.

"Perhaps you can come again. One more time. I don't want to upset Teresa needlessly," says the Mother Superior. "There were so many orphaned Jewish children in those days," she says on our way back. "Left in our care to grow up as Catholics. What else could we do?"

"You could have told them the truth," I venture.

Mother Superior looks at me somewhat mockingly.

"And then what? After the war they had no families left to bring them up. Jewish people left Poland by the thousands. How could we nuns give these children a Jewish upbringing?"

In a way I see her point. "But what of the poor children, never knowing who they really are?" I ask.

"I can tell you," says the Mother Superior, avoiding my

question, "that I have always suspected the child Teresa is Jewish. I will try to find out more and let you know."

I give her my hotel address and telephone number in Warsaw.

She eyes me suspiciously now. "What is a young girl like you doing here? It's dangerous. The Communists hate foreigners. You should be home with your parents, not running around this country chasing butterfly dreams, my daughter."

I say goodbye politely, glad that I am not her daughter, and go back into the waiting room to join the others.

Soon the three of us are speeding down the road toward Warsaw, while I brief my friends on the meeting with Teresa.

"She looks a little like my sister," I insist, then open my purse to look at the photograph once more. It's not there. Not in any of the compartments!

Teresa did not give it back, and I forgot all about it.

The Revelation

The three of us return to Warsaw full of anticipation.

The next day it rains and a heavy mood descends upon us. Tad telephones to say that he has some business to attend to. Mur is moping around because his reading at the university has been postponed without explanation. I return to my room after breakfast and decide to read for a while, although my mind is a beehive of thoughts, centred on Teresa, Basia, and Mortynski.

I reread Babushka's letter and play with the gold pendant. As I turn it around in my hand it springs open. I didn't realize that this was a locket. Inside there is a picture of a beautiful young girl. She has small features, and her face is framed in ringlets. This mysterious girl must be my Aunt Luda, who died of pneumonia at the age of thirteen. On the other side of the locket is a Star of David.

Someone knocks. A piece of paper slides underneath the door into my room. I grab it quickly and see that it's a message from the Mother Superior. In one sentence, she tells me to come to the convent as soon as possible.

I run back to the restaurant and find Mur still at the breakfast table, reading the *Warsaw Courier*.

Mur looks up and sees the concern in my face. "You look distraught," he comments. I tell him about the note.

"Tadeusz told me yesterday," Mur explains, "after we got back from the convent, that he can't go back there for party reasons. The SB is watching all of us closely." Mur butts out his cigarette. Lately he's been smoking like a burnt-down building.

I panic. "How will we get there without Tad driving us?"

"Tell you what," Mur says cheerfully, "you and I will get on a train and go there ourselves, what do you say?"

I breathe more easily. I love being with Mur. He is sensitive and consistent, and makes me feel secure. I run back to my room and stuff the red file into my bag.

In just over an hour, we are back at the convent. We ring. Sister Ursula greets us. Her jovial, full-cheeked face is flushed as she ushers me into the Mother Superior's office.

The Mother Superior is sitting behind her desk looking stern in her steel-rimmed glasses. I sit down in the chair opposite.

"Last evening," she begins, "after you left, I had a talk with one of the sisters here who lived and worked at Holy Trinity convent, where Teresa stayed before she came here. She told me that Teresa was brought there by a man who is her uncle and who had rescued her from the Gestapo. Teresa is a Jewish child, or I should say, was.

She has become Catholic."

"Then she could be my sister?"

"Don't raise your hopes too high," warns the Mother Superior, casting a shadow on my hopefulness.

"Who was the man that rescued her?"

"Teresa will tell you herself," she says. "She is one of hundreds of children who share this fate."

I am trying to understand her new attitude and why she is trying to help.

"Teresa looks like my grandmother as a young girl," I tell her, remembering Babushka's portrait that hung in Papa's library, above his chair behind the desk. I show her the picture of my aunt inside the locket. There is definitely a resemblance.

"I understand you wanting this," says the Mother Superior, scrutinizing the small picture. "I also know that memory can sometimes be exaggerated, when one hopes for a dream to come true. Besides, you were so young when it all happened. This picture may or may not resemble Teresa. It's hard to tell."

I am so tired of being told that I was only a child during the war, so how can I possibly remember what happened. Of course my early memory, up until the age of five, could just be wishful thinking. But after that I know it's practically indisputable. I made a firm decision some time ago not to be a person who conveniently blocks out sad truths.

"May I see Teresa again, alone?" I ask, using up my last ounce of courage and self-assurance.

The Mother Superior shifts uncomfortably in her chair.

"I would feel bad denying you this favour," she says. "But I can allow you only a very short visit. Half an hour at the most."

"Thank you, thank you so much," I blurt out with gratitude.

I follow her silently once again down the familiar corridor. The building, in its sparseness, has the chill of a stony cave. As always, certain sounds, smells and objects bring up those early memories of war. I listen to our footsteps echoing eerily down the hall, and I am reminded of Nazi boots stomping through the hallways of ghetto buildings during their raids. Surely not here? But then, Nazis hunted Jews everywhere, even in convents.

We enter the library. The Mother Superior instructs one of the sisters to get Teresa. If only I knew how to conduct myself. How to approach Teresa? How to get at the truth? I do not know how to tackle this serious business alone, even with the help of Tad and Mur.

After some time, Teresa walks into the room looking more transparent and fragile than yesterday. Her eyes zoom toward me. They remind me of my mother's eyes. Her hair, of my aunt's ringlets in the photograph inside the locket. Or is my imagination in overdrive?

The Mother Superior tactfully informs us that she'll return in half an hour. I look at my watch in order to pace myself. Now that we're alone, my head is in a daze. I can't seem to concentrate.

Half an hour to solve years of agony of not knowing. Of the anguish that could have been avoided had we known the truth.

We behold each other questioningly. Are we sisters, or am I chasing a shadow?

"Do you have the photograph?" I ask finally.

Teresa takes something out of her side pocket, a handkerchief folded around a square object. It's the photograph. She looks at it for a long time.

"I don't know," she says eventually. "I don't know. I don't remember. This girl just looks so familiar." She hands back the picture. Her eyes fall on the locket around my neck and stay there.

"Tell me what happened to you after the war, when you were old enough to remember," I query, feeling desperately inept at this.

"He..." she begins quietly. "He used to tie me to the doorknob when he went out, and would leave his vicious dog to sit nearby. Each time I kicked up a fuss the dog would snarl. I hated that dog. The woman, his wife, was afraid of him too. I was glad to have left that house. In the convent I felt safer, though I'd have given anything to have a home and family."

Who is he, the man? I wonder, then reach quickly into the file in my purse for a photograph of Mortynski.

"Do you recognize this photograph?"

She stops fingering the rosary and takes the photo. One look at it and she quickly crosses herself. "It's my uncle," she whispered. "Uncle Mort."

Papa once told me that Mortynski was very strict with Basia, though he said he loved her like his own daughter. So how did he get to be Teresa's uncle?

She doesn't remember how.

I show her a picture of Mama and Papa. She shakes her head. "I don't know these people," she says, helpless tears welling up in her brilliant eyes.

There is this great urge to hug her and to comfort her. Instead I listen as she composes herself and goes on. I listen for any clue, any tiny thing that would indicate that she could be my sister.

"My mother had a locket like this one," she says abruptly.

It can't be the same one, I think. It's impossible. Mama never wore this locket. And even if Mortynski is Teresa's uncle, her story could be that of any child orphaned during the war. The abandonment. Moments of terror. The unbelonging. Both the cruelty and kindness on the part of those who were rescuers. The missing links like the locket or a photograph.

It's the story of a wartime child, who because of her young age only remembers fragments.

"Do you know if you are Jewish?" I say. A vague expression crosses Teresa's face.

"I am a Catholic now," she states. "It doesn't matter what I was before."

The curtain falls. Even if this is my sister, a fact that I can't prove as yet, she is probably lost to us now. Anna's words echo in my head, "Forget about Basia." Forget, forget, forget.

"After the war, I too had great difficulties in coming to terms with my Jewishness," I confess, trying to find a thread of communication.

Teresa just looks down into her lap. Her delicate hands

finger the rosary with conviction and knowing. Her face lights up with each touch as if something mysterious was passing between her and the beads.

Suddenly she looks up and stares again at the locket around my neck.

I take it off and show it to her. "Who is this beautiful girl?" she asks in a very soft voice.

"It's my aunt, Luda. Look at her hair. It's just like yours." I tell her the rest quickly.

"What is this star?" she asks.

"It's the Jewish national emblem. The Star of David, King of Israel."

Teresa fingers the emblem, looking mystified as she hands me back the locket. At that instant, the Mother Superior enters with another nun. The half-hour is up.

Teresa says goodbye, then hesitates. She comes slowly toward me and puts her little arms around me. I hug her. She pulls back and stares again long and hard at the locket.

I feel something being slipped into my pocket. Teresa kisses me on the cheek and runs out of the library.

"Strange behaviour," says Mother Superior. "She definitely looks unhappy," she adds, sounding displeased.

"I found out that her uncle is the same man who was hiding my sister Basia," I tell her.

The nun doesn't even flinch. "I am not surprised, and neither should you be. It's well known that Mortynski hid a number of families with small children during the war, for money of course. Not all survived. Apparently his brother had married a Jewish woman, Teresa's mother, who was sent to a concentration camp. They say his brother, a Catholic, was taken to Auschwitz for having married a Jew. But who knows?"

She'd known the story all along, yet she'd led me on.

"I am sorry, but yours has not been the first inquiry of this sort, and it won't be the last."

I take the locket off my neck, open it, and hand it over to her. "Please look at it again," I beg.

She examines it in silence.

"A small resemblance in the hair," she admits.

The Mother Superior hands me back the locket and gets up from her chair. The visit is over.

I am disappointed. All my excitement and hope of finding Basia are in shreds.

We walk back in silence. The doors close behind the Mother Superior as she enters her office. I place my hand in the pocket of my dress and find a photograph of Teresa. On the back she wrote:

Dear Slava,

Please show this photograph to your mother.
Love
Teresa

Mur and I walk out of the convent and down the road toward the train station.

I tell him what happened.

"There will be always a tinge of doubt left," says Mur resolutely, on our way back to Warsaw.

He knows. What happened to Basia will haunt me forever. And Teresa will remain a question mark. Having been so young when it all happened, she has no memory of the past. Maybe Mama will know if this girl could be Basia.

The train speeds through a peaceful landscape, but the landscape of my soul is in turmoil. I can't get Teresa's green eyes and pale, fragile face out of my mind and heart. What if she is Basia, after all?

The Official

"You look worn out. Where have you two been?" inquires Tad, back at the hotel. He looks alarmed and distraught. So unlike him.

"I've bad news," he continues, without waiting for us to answer. "The security agents are after us, and I can't shake them off."

"Oh, oh, the Polish KGB," says Mur with concern. "Why are they after us?"

"Mortynski knows we are looking for Basia. But when he found out that we went to the convent and were snooping around a girl that I found out is his niece, he probably hit the roof. Besides that, we were seen at Zofia's, who knows too much about him. I am pretty sure that's why he had us followed."

How could he have found out all this so fast?

"So, what?" I say flippantly, "we've done nothing to him...yet."

"That's not the point," replies Tad impatiently. "He is

making up lies. Like saying that you two are spies. You know the kind of a person he is."

"To stay away from!" says Mur emphatically.

This is all my fault. I dragged them into this situation.

"If you hadn't offered your help, I would have never asked to come here!" I say defensively.

"Too late now!" exclaims Tad. "You two should leave Poland on the next plane to London, before they take you in for questioning, or throw you out, if you're lucky. Maybe that's why the university has delayed your reading, Andrzej."

Mur shrugs his shoulders. He doesn't seem to care much about the reading.

"This doesn't sound good," he says. "Do you mean to say that they could keep us here?"

"Indefinitely. If they suspect something."

"I am a British subject. Slava is Canadian, which is a similar thing," says Mur more seriously now.

"To them you're Poles. Go upstairs and pack, we're leaving for the airport immediately," orders Tad.

"What about our passports?" asks Mur. "We have to get them back from the desk clerk."

"Let me handle those. Meet me at my car in forty-five minutes."

Horrible thoughts rattle my brain as I run up the stairs to my room. Persecuted again! For what?

I throw everything into the suitcase except the Lenski File, which I put into my little travel bag.

Forty-five minutes later, we're on our way to Tad's car.

"Your passports have been withheld," says Tad, visibly perplexed. "We're leaving anyhow."

He places the luggage in the trunk and, as Mur and I are about to get in the car, two men in black leather coats approach us.

One, short and fat, takes Mur's arm and the other, tall and burly, grabs mine.

"Let's go," barks the tall and burly one in Polish with a Russian accent.

They lead us to a black car, which I instantly recognize as the one that has been following us. They push us into it. Tall and burly goes over to Tad, who has just slammed the trunk on his car with our luggage inside it. Tall and burly hauls the luggage out of Tad's car and puts it in the black car.

He speaks to Tad in a hushed voice. Tad gets into his car and drives away.

"Tad's a traitor," I hiss to Mur.

Mur says nothing. The look in his eyes tells me to be silent. Tall and burly gets behind the wheel. He drives like a maniac, swearing at anyone who gets in his way. The words are in vulgar Russian. Shorty sits between me and Mur, squeezing up against my thighs. There is no room for me to move away.

We stop in front of a grey building that has Polish and Russian flags in front, and several uniformed men on guard at the entrance.

Escorted by the two men, we walk up several flights of stairs, along a dimly lit corridor, and into an office. Tall and burly yells, "Sit!"

Just like Mortynski talking to his dogs.

He disappears into another office, while the little fat man keeps vigil.

After a short while, the other man returns and roughly takes Mur and me by the arms.

"Into that office," he barks again, pushing us through the door and into two chairs opposite a dirty mahogany desk.

The man at the desk looks grim and very official. He wears a dark suit, white shirt, and a beige tie. His hair is black. It has that glued-back, shiny look. His head is the shape of a vertical ellipse. His eyes are steel-grey and expressionless. His fingers are wide-knuckled and wiry. They look cruel, clamp-like. Like fingers that crush butterflies and later pin the dead specimens onto a board behind glass.

The air is thick with danger. It's hard to breathe.

"Your passports," demands the official. He glares at Mur and me. The tall and burly man takes our passports out of his pocket, and hands them to the official.

The official takes his time. He reads and rereads the passports, turning the pages as if scanning an exam paper. He flips the pages back and forth, probing, studying every detail.

After a while, he looks at me sceptically.

"What are you, a young lady, doing here in Warsaw?" he asks, placing a tinge of sarcasm on the word "lady."

"I came here as an assistant to Tadeusz Skovronek," I reply. My voice sounds clear and defiant. Suddenly I am no longer afraid. I've done nothing wrong. Instead, these men and this place fill me with loathing. I am no longer a helpless child in the war. Now I am grown up and ready to defy anyone who wants to harm me.

The official makes an ugly face, as if he'd heard my thoughts.

"An assistant! An assistant to what?"

"In languages, particularly English and Polish. I can also speak Russian."

The official's ears perk up.

"I translate well from one to the other," I add.

"And you, Comrade Mur, what is your business here?"

Mur explains that he was invited to read a paper on Maxim Gorky at the University of Warsaw.

"Commendable," says the official. "So you're an intellectual," he adds, mockery spread all over his face like peanut butter on a bun.

Without further comment, he pushes a button on his desk. A buzz can be heard in the outer office. A woman enters. She is pretty, sort of military looking, with shortly cropped brown hair, and a stout figure moulded into a brown dress with brass buttons.

"Bring in Comrade Mortynski," commands the official.

"Yes, Comrade," she answers coquettishly, "right away."

The woman marches away and returns immediately with the man I detest: Mortynski.

He stands at the desk next to the official, looking down at us. Sure of himself, as if he owned the world.

He makes me think of Hitler.

"What do you have to say, Comrade Mortynski, about

these people?" queries the official.

Mortynski stares straight at me. "I believe that this girl and this man," he says, pointing to Mur, "are British spies." His voice has an unpleasant rattle to it.

I can't believe his words! This is the continuing vendetta between him and my father.

"I also think," he adds, "that Comrade Tadeusz is innocent of all this."

The slime. He even goes as far as to vindicate Tadeusz, because he has a high position in the party. Of course, to save his own neck.

"Take them downstairs," orders the official.

They grab Mur and me and practically push us down the stairs. They throw me into a room in the cellar, taking Mur away with them.

The cell is full of women. They stare at me suspiciously. A scraggly older woman comes forward, screeching, "And what have you done?" I say nothing. A tough-looking girl of Amazon height pushes me into the corner, isolating me from the rest. She stands in front of me like a soldier, ogling. Several other women are lying on dirty narrow mattresses scattered about with moth-eaten, stained blankets. Others lean against the wall and stare into space.

Smelly bedpans line one wall. The cell walls are concrete. There are rusted iron bars outside the windows overlooking a grey facade streaked with light from the street above.

The cell stinks of mould and urine.

The Amazon points me to a mattress in the corner. I

sink onto it and sit there. I don't know for how long.

It's getting dark outside. A bald light bulb on the ceiling casts a ghostly light on the grey walls and the unkempt women with dirty faces and greasy hair. I feel cold and I am getting desperate. What to do?

Suddenly, for a split second, the door opens and slams shut. Someone pushes in a tray with a glass of murky water and a blob of stale black bread. It sits on the dusty floor, fare for mice.

"That's for her," says the older woman, pushing the tray in my direction with her foot. I bite into the blob. Its hardened crust cuts into my lip, making it bleed. I eat a few crumbs. I sip the water, which tastes like mud. Exhausted, I lie down on the stinking mattress again, and close my eyes. I try not to think of Tadeusz, and what a complete rat he'd turned out to be.

There is a body next to me, bundled up in a blanket. Someone in there is stirring. A face emerges. It's bloody under the eyes, and bruised. She looks at me with brown eyes, their bloodied eyeballs ringed by bluish bruises. She tells me her name is Gosia, then whispers, "They don't like foreigners here. These women are not all bad, but you look like a foreigner, so they feel spied on."

I shrug my shoulders. What can I do about that? I thought I looked as Polish as the rest. But I guess I don't. I feel sorry for the woman, Gosia. She tells me through dry, cracked lips that she's been badly beaten for refusing to sign a document that would force her to tell a lie about a friend who did nothing but take some photographs of ships in the harbour.

I offer what little water I have left. She takes it willingly. The others look on. There is no hostility in their eyes, only pity for poor Gosia.

I fall into a feverish sleep. The turkey nightmare comes back for the first time since St. Anne's Boarding School. *The turkey is enormous and lunges at me with its claws. There are hundreds of them screeching around me, coming toward me, closer and closer. I smell the stench of their droppings...*

I wake up and need to pass water. I crawl over the sleeping bodies, toward the nearest bedpan. There is no paper. I use the corner of my slip, then try to rinse it with the drop of water left in my bowl. My mouth feels like an outhouse. Something scurries against the wall and squeaks. It's a rat.

They've even taken away my bag with the toothbrush, comb and what's worse, the Lenski File. If I came back here to find the past, I got more than I bargained for. This is what it was like to be imprisoned in the Warsaw ghetto and persecuted for no reason. But there is one thing different now. I am not as afraid.

16
Scarface

Time passes, vanishing into the grey wall of the cell. The women here, I find out from my neighbour Gosia, have been jailed mostly because of their associations with suspected spies. She informs me that most of these women are hard. Some are prostitutes, some are thieves. All have had a tough life, working hard and being poor. A few have kind hearts.

Gosia is feeling better today. I try to look after her. She points out a woman, Magda, whose job it is to inform on the rest of us. Magda has privileges. She gets food and soup and water to drink, a better mattress, and clean bedding. The other women are afraid of her and treat her with quiet contempt.

With each minute I grow more despondent and my bravado thins. All I can do in this state is engage my thinking gear.

If I seek help from the Canadian government they'll notify Mama and Max, who will punish me for the rest of

145

my life. Maybe that's better than suffering here. How could I have ever trusted Tadeusz? Even in London he proved to be a total scoundrel.

The cell door opens.

"Lenska!" commands a stout, dour-looking woman. It must be my turn.

"Come with me!" orders the woman. She takes me roughly by the arm, pinching my flesh, and escorts me out into the corridor and up the stairs. Maybe they're letting me go.

We enter a dimly lit room. There is a desk with two chairs in a shadowy corner, and in another corner, a sink with a hose attached to the tap. A man's silhouette stands inert in front of the narrow window. Suddenly a sharp light goes on. It blinds me. The man, in a military uniform, emerges from the shadows. He places one foot on the chair. He is smoking a cigarette.

"Sit down, sit down, please," he says in a gentle voice. There is a long scar on his right cheek.

"You may go," he orders the woman, flinging his arm toward her as if he were fighting off an insect.

My thin, half-torn clothes are hardly enough to protect me from the pervasive dampness of this room. I tremble but try my darndest not to let it show.

The man's dark eyes bore into me like cockroaches.

They make my skin crawl.

"A runaway from home looking for adventure," he mocks. "Or an innocent little British translator spying on the activities of the Socialist Party's agents. Which is it now, little girl?"

In the light of the lamp, his scar makes him look like a character in the *Phantom Of The Opera*, a film I'd seen not so long ago.

"Neither," I reply somewhat weakly.

"Don't you get cheeky with me!" The gentle voice suddenly becomes harsh. "What is your connection with Zofia Soplinska?"

I shake my head in disbelief. What has she got to do with all this?

"If you talk. Tell the truth. It'll be easier on you."

The smoke cloud that flows around me from his cigarette is thick and nauseating. A pile of half-smoked butts smoulders in a dirty ashtray on the desk.

"I repeat, what is your connection with Zofia Soplinska of Honey Street?"

"I knew her as a child. My grandmother lived across the road."

"Easy story. I don't believe you. Now you tell me the truth or I'll whip it out of you."

He lights another cigarette then proceeds to take off his belt.

"Lie on the floor with your face down," he orders.

I lie down with my face on my hands, trying not to touch the filthy floor. It smells of excrement and urine. People must have lost control in this room. Small wonder, I think, desperately trying not to pee.

I have nothing to say. Whatever he is accusing me of is false.

The strap crashes down on my back. It stings and burns. Once, twice and again. I bite my hand in a bid to stifle a moan. Everything goes black.

I come to in that chair. I can hardly breathe. My back feels broken.

"I am giving you another chance to answer," barks Scarface.

"I tell you, Mortynski is an evil man," I murmur. My voice sounds as if it were coming from behind an iron mask. "He was a Nazi during the war, conspiring against the Polish state. He wouldn't give back my sister after the war..." I proceed to tell the whole story about Basia.

Scarface stands motionless, posed like a predator observing his prey. For a brief moment, something akin to human crosses his face, then leaves, returning it to stone.

He goes slowly over to the sink, picks up the hose and drags it over to my chair.

"You can be severely punished for spreading such lies! Tell the truth!" he shouts.

I say nothing more.

He throws the hose on the floor and goes back to the sink. He turns on the tap.

The water hisses onto the floor. He picks up the hose and points it at me. It's a long snake threatening to pounce.

"The truth," he yells.

"I've already told you the truth," I mumble, leaning back in fear.

Suddenly he turns the hose on my face. It gushes into my nose, my mouth, my eyes. Again, I can't breathe. I can't breathe. The water hits my body with icy, frenetic power. First my chest and shoulders, then my midriff, then back onto my face. I am drowning. I am dying...

When I come to, I am lying on a mattress. My body is a block of ice. There are wet rags sticking to me. All over me. Take them off. There is a familiar face bending over me. Am I dreaming? It's Zofia! I try to speak but nothing comes out of my mouth. I feel weak...

"Don't speak, child," says Zofia's voice. She is pulling the wet rags off me and covering me up with rough blankets. I am shivering. I am surprised to be alive.

Zofia lies down next to me, trying to comfort me with her body. Once again, I remember her kindness to me during the war. She tells me how they came to take her away, and about Mortynski's accusations. Her tired voice drifts off and she sleeps.

Many more hours pass. Zofia doesn't move. She must be asleep. Women's voices whisper stories, weeping, swearing. Zofia still hasn't moved. Semi-delirious, I reach out and touch her. She is cold.

"Gosia," I whisper to my neighbour. "Look at this woman next to me, please," I beg her.

Gosia cries out, "She's dead! She's dead!"

I cradle Zofia's head with my arm. Everything dims.

I feel cold water on my head. I hear a voice.

"Give this to Lenska." It's the guard. Someone places a tray on my belly. A blob of black bread and murky water. I've seen this before.

"Eat, or you'll die from starvation," whispers Gosia. She is still pale and sickly-looking. Still lying on the floor, covered up with a flea-bitten blanket. She is coughing now, non-stop. It's very damp here. A woman comes by occasionally and douses the cell floor with water to clean it. All our belongings get wet and hardly ever dry out. Suddenly I remember. Zofia was here and now she is dead. She died. I heard them say it. Poor, kind Zofia. Soon they come and take her body away. I am beyond feeling. I listen half-heartedly to Gosia's whisperings going on as if nothing had happened.

"My boyfriend, whom I told you about, was just taking those photos for fun," says Gosia wistfully. "Now they're telling me that he was spying on the navy. He should have known that cameras are forbidden in public places. They beat me on the face so I'd admit that he is a spy, then they say I'll get off. A lie is truth around here."

Just like during the war. When you had to lie about who you were in order to live.

I pick up the bread, determined to survive. There is a piece of paper tucked into the dough, which splits in two. The women are busy talking. Only Gosia could have seen it, but her eyes are closed now. I hide the paper under the blanket and quickly read the typewritten words.

Zofia is in prison. M. told lies about her associations
with foreigners who were spies, meaning you. I have
your papers. Don't worry,
The poet

A message from Tad. He is on our side after all. If he only knew that Zofia is dead!

I try to eat the bread with a dry mouth, then fall into a heavy sleep.

I wake up coughing, and continue coughing until

morning. I've wet my bed because I have no strength to get up and use the facility in the corner. I tear Tad's letter to shreds, and stuff them into a hole in the mattress. Night falls.

In the morning, Gosia tells the other women to call a guard to come and see me.

"This girl is very sick," they tell him.

Some hours later a doctor comes and takes my temperature. He tells the guard that I have a bad case of pneumonia and must be hospitalized. He reminds the guard that I am a Canadian, and that they could get into a lot of trouble if they allow me to die. The guard snickers and leaves, but later comes back with three other men and a stretcher. One of them is Scarface. I am placed in a van. Its motion spins me into a feverish dream.

There are ruins everywhere. Poles armed with axes, saws, and hammers are repairing a sick city. Warsaw. Collecting shrapnel, unexploded bombs, and clearing away bricks that lie scattered across the streets. They lift a streetcar up onto the damaged rails. I wait and wait for it to start moving. The doors swing open.

I have a pocket full of pennies, with which I am going to pay the conductor, but a mob of pushing, shoving people sweeps me onto the streetcar. It is fire-engine red. Red in and out, glossy red like Mama's nail polish. People hang onto the streetcar door handles and dangle off them, their bodies half in and half out. I am squeezed between two men who fall against me each time the streetcar sways. It stops and a little girl gets out. Through the window I see her walking away and getting smaller. There is a gold locket around her neck, my locket. It's Basia. "Basia! Wait for me!" I scream without a voice. "Wait!" She disappears. I can't get out. I am wedged between these men, who are drunken soldiers. There is vodka on their breath. Its pungent smell penetrates my eyes nose and throat. Basia had disappeared again. I am in despair. These men want sex. They begin to take off my blouse. I struggle. Further down in the streetcar, there are other soldiers, raping screaming women. Everything is a brilliant glossy red, like blood.

I wake up in the hospital and see Tad's face leaning toward me.

I tell him about Zofia.

I feel guilty. We shouldn't have involved her in my affairs. "It's all my fault!" I cry, feeling weak and powerless.

Tad shakes his head sadly. "Zofia is the typical victim of this system," he whispers. "She is the scapegoat. They had to blame someone. Her son told me she had a weak heart, and that's what she died of in your cell."

"I want to go to the funeral!" I say angrily. "I must go!"

"Are you mad? This is no time for melodrama, Slava. Get a hold of yourself, if you want to survive this. Going anywhere near Zofia now could implicate you further with Mortynski."

"We've already gone too far, Tad. There proves to be more to all this than looking for my lost sister." Tad tries to pacify me. Nothing helps. What I thought was going to be a private search for Basia is leaving a trail of tragedy behind. For the first time since I left Vancouver and Canada, I wish I were back there in safety, peace, and above all, freedom.

17
Bittersweet

Tadeusz is worried.

"There is trouble ahead," he tells me. "Until we can prove Mortynski guilty of lies and murder, you're also the scapegoat, the guilty party. That's how the system works. Mur has been released—he is considered a hero because he killed Nazis while fighting for Poland. Besides, he has valid proof from the University of Warsaw of why he was here. They wouldn't let him read his paper on Gorky, though, and they've sent him back to England."

With Mur gone, I don't feel safe. I miss his reassuring presence.

Today my body feels like a broken engine: weak and useless, although my temperature has gone down somewhat. Tad tells me I've been here three days. I think I'd rather stay sick than go back to that prison.

I can't absorb the fact that I may be to blame for Zofia's death. That I have killed her! Tad has different theories about this.

He thinks he is so smart, but one question has plagued my mind for days.

"How do you keep out of all this?" I dare to ask.

"What keeps me immune in this case," he answers thoughtfully, "is a family connection. My uncle on the Russian side of the family, with whom I have an excellent relationship, is a high-ranking Soviet official. Because of this they don't touch me. But who knows how long this privilege may last..." Tad breaks off and stares out the dirty window.

"I think I've found a hole in the tapestry." He embarks on a theory. "I am certain that Mortynski informed on Zofia because she knew too much. Didn't she say she saw him digging up the jewellery? If it were known that Mortynski is a rich Party member, that might raise some eyebrows. But we need something else. He must have some questionable foreign connections that would make him an undesirable here."

"Mortynski's greed may take him to dangerous people outside of the party," I offer.

"I showed the Lenski File to the official," Tad says distractedly, dismissing my idea, "who had your passport, to prove that Mortynski was a scoundrel, but he didn't quite believe it because the signatures on the papers were faded and barely legible. Besides, the Polish Court had already cleared Mortynski of your father's accusations. I found out, though, that Mortynski is not that popular lately with the Party members. They won't tell me why.

"If I found the people whose names your father mentioned in the file, they could testify against Mortynski.

That would, at the very least, get us more proof against him.

"There is one more ace in the hole," he adds, smiling mischievously. "I know our official's deep, dark secret. He is trying to cover up an affair with the wife of a Russian dignitary in Krakow who is higher in rank than our official himself!"

"Tadeusz," I say horrified. "You're a blackmailer like Mortynski!"

"I am doing all this not for the love of money, but to save you from disaster."

What can I say to that? I know Tad is really trying to help, but at the same time I have difficulty dealing with his conspiratorial nature.

"So what next?" I ask.

He tells me that we must wait until my temperature completely subsides before we can take action.

Several days later, at dawn, Tad comes to the hospital with a long raincoat to cover up my torn, dirty clothes. We sneak out by the back stairs. The soldier guarding my room has been bribed and pretends to be asleep.

We get into Tad's borrowed car and speed out of Warsaw.

Now that we're alone, I find the strength to tell Tad what they did to me, and about Scarface's cruel tactics. He puts his arm around me protectively.

"I am sorry. It must have been terrible for you. They constantly use torture on suspected spies to get information. I tried to spare you as much as I possibly could. Dubin, or Scarface as you've named him, has a terrible reputation for this. He has no feelings."

He slows down in front of a big country house.

"It's a getaway," he explains, "where high officials hold secret meetings. Some spend time here with their mistresses. I have a key to a room with a separate entrance."

"By the way, look." Tad pulls a leather pouch from his inside jacket pocket, dangling it in front of me. My pouch! Quickly I look inside, and find, to my great relief, the red file, folded in half.

"I rescued it from the men who took it away from you, in order to show these papers to the Official. I also have your suitcase and your small bag. Later I'll tell you my plan."

Tad parks deep among the trees behind the house so the car is hidden from the road. He takes my suitcase out of the trunk and leads me to a door that opens onto a single flight of stairs. I climb the steps with difficulty, then enter a room whose windows look out on a peaceful field with a forest beyond. The air that wafts in smells of moist earth, grass, and manure. I remember when I first smelled the French Canadian country air and thought then how it reminded me of a Polish field like this one.

I am hiding again, like the fugitive Jews who ran from village to village to escape their Nazi predators.

Tad opens a bottle of wine and gives me some bread and cheese.

A dog howls somewhere.

Tad turns on the radio to drown out the howling. Soft music comes on. The atmosphere is becoming similar to the one in London, the night I fell in love with him.

"We haven't had much time together these last few weeks," says Tad gently.

That nameless feeling comes over me again. I thought I was too numb to feel anything. Surely it's been all over between us for a long while. He told me so before in no uncertain terms. Now I need to think and be alone. To reflect. To get out of my rags. I take out a change of clothes and go to wash up.

In the washroom, I feel safer from the nagging question of Tad and the problems of my escape. The water is cold. I cringe as it hits my body. Memory of that day with Scarface and the downpour of water that whipped my body and face comes back in a chilly torrent. I will never take another shower as long as I live!

I dry myself with a rough towel, then look in the mirror, thinking of Tad's many women friends.

> Mirror, mirror on the wall
> Who is the prettiest of them all?

I don't find myself pretty. I don't even like my body, with its rounded hips and small breasts that resemble fried eggs, sunny side up.

Chilled to the bone, but clean, I dress and return to the room. My wine glass has been filled. I sip the wine, and soon begin to feel warmer.

Tad looks at me as if he were seeing me for the first time.

"Would you like to stay in Poland and live here?"

Just like that! The question hits me like the cold water. He must be joking!

"If things were normal here as they are in America, maybe I would." My answer is surprisingly quick but matter-of-fact. I am not ready to change my life that drastically. Besides, has he forgotten that I am still a prisoner of the Polish Security Department? Ironically, I am his prisoner, too.

"You're a beautiful girl," he says softly.

Why does he have to choose such an inauspicious moment for compliments, even if they do make me feel good? Besides, I am now attracted to Tad in a way that feels more like friendship.

He comes around to my chair. Puts both his arms around me and kisses me. It's different than before. He seems softer, more loving. Unsure of my feelings, but desperately longing for affection, I submit to his protective presence. We rest together inside the night's silent shell, transient like chrysalides.

The Rescue Mission

It's dawn. Sounds of male and female voices outside.

Tadeusz wakes from sleep and moans all the way to the window, trying to see who is there, then opens the door.

I throw on my housecoat.

A man and woman stand on the threshold. Tad invites them in.

"Mrs. Mira and Mr. Mietek Richtman," he introduces us formally, "meet Slava Lenska, my friend, who has a lot of information about Roman Mortynski."

We shake hands and sit down around the table, still strewn with wine glasses and breadcrumbs from the night before.

"I knew your father," says Mr. Richtman, turning to me. "He was a good, honest man. He suffered greatly when he had to go against his principles to save his family. Just as most of us had to do, lie about who we were." Mrs. Richtman's face is sad as she nods in confirmation of her husband's statement.

"When Mr. Skovronek called and asked us to meet him here, I didn't want to at first. But we'll do anything to expose what Mortynski did to us. Wouldn't we, Mietek?" says Mrs. Richtman.

Mr. Richtman seems lost in deep thought. "Yes. We feel it our duty, even though we are afraid of repercussions. But I am also doing this for Stefan Lenski who was my friend, and who shared his last crumb of bread with me during the war."

So Papa and Mr. Richtman really were friends. It feels good to meet someone who knew Papa. I want to ask Tad how he got the Richtmans over here, but I guess it's not important now. Thank God they could be found.

Tad takes my file out of the leather pouch, leafs through it, and pulls out a sheet of paper.

"The entry here states that Mortynski blackmailed you for your property and possessions after he gave you a place to hide from the Nazis."

The Richtmans nod in accord.

"Would you be willing to testify that Mortynski was a Nazi collaborator?" asks Tad with great self-assurance.

The Richtmans look at one another.

"You said that all you needed was a letter. I have a hard time believing that Jewish testimony would make a difference in a Polish court of law," says Mrs. Richtman, sounding upset.

Her husband pats her hand. "My wife is right. The Poles have no great love for us Jews. My sister was killed in the Kielce incident. You know of that massacre in 1946, don't you?"

"I never heard of it. It probably happened right after we'd left Poland," I reply.

Mr. Richtman explains.

"On July 4th, 1946, after the liberation of Poland, my sister went to Kielce to visit a cousin. As they were sitting in the cousin's apartment drinking tea, some people burst through the doors and hit my sister on the neck with a spade. Instant death. The cousin ran from the room and escaped, unharmed, through the back door of the building.

"The whole incident began when a young boy came home after being absent for a few days. He told his father that Jews had detained him, when in reality he had been at a friend's home all that time. It was a lie invented by the boy's friend to make the Poles think that Jews were stealing Christian children to use them for ritualistic purposes. An incensed mob of Poles then gathered and massacred around forty-two Jews of Kielce."[*]

The story is beyond comprehension. Just like what happened to our people during the war. "How could they do this?" I cry out.

"Thousands of Jews left Poland after that," remarks Mrs. Richtman.

"There are very few of us left in Poland now, though once there were three million. That's why we are afraid to attract attention," adds her husband.

"We mustn't let a possible double agent like Mortynski deceive the state any longer. Besides, he blackmailed Jewish people and may still be doing it," interjects Tad.

---

* See Reference p. 216

"Why would you, an ardent Party member, insist on this justice being done?" Mr. Richtman asks Tad.

"There are those of us who believe in justice," insists Tad, "and want criminals to be punished, regardless of their rank in the Party. All you need to do is sign this letter, which I can use as evidence against Mortynski. I can promise that nothing bad will happen to you. Your testimony can also free this innocent young girl, who may otherwise be held under suspicion and not allowed to return to Canada.

"You don't need to be present in court," explains Tad. "The reason I asked you to come here is that we had no time to come to you. Please sign here at the bottom." Tad pushes a written statement toward the Richtmans.

After reading the document and exchanging some words in Yiddish between themselves, the Richtmans agree to sign.

I thank them. They give me their address in Falenica and leave.

Tad and I are left alone again.

He comes close and puts his arm around me. "I do care for you, Slava, don't worry," he whispers. "The Richtmans' testimony will help us to convince the party that Mortynski is a trickster who is not to be trusted.

"Listen to me," he continues in a harsher tone of voice. "There is a plane I want you to be on, leaving for London in five hours. But first I have to go back to Warsaw with these papers. I have to see the Official and have him release your passport." I resent his harshness, his sudden change of mood. And yet he is trying to get me out of here. Why do I feel so ungrateful?

"You'll have to stay here and wait."

"What about Teresa? What about my sister? Maybe I need to search more, elsewhere?"

"Slava, you may never know. Teresa doesn't remember, and Mortynski will not tell you unless forced to by the authorities. You can't afford to wait this out in Poland. I will try to look further for your sister. I promise that when Mortynski's case comes up I will get on it. I will keep in touch with the Mother Superior and I will write you about everything, I promise."

Having said his piece, Tad leaves.

Can I believe him? I so want to believe him. At least I have found someone here who can be on the lookout for Basia in case she is still alive.

I turn on the radio and lie down, feeling drowsy.

There are people rattling their weapons outside the house. Women are crying, holding onto their babies. Where am I? A man runs in with a gun. He is wearing a Nazi uniform. Oh, no. It's happening again, I hide in a closet and see another man in a Polish uniform take a baby out of its mother's arms and hold it up to an open window. The baby disappears. I hear whisperings from women huddling in corners. "A Jew, a Jewish child."

A rustling noise wakes me up. I am thankful that it was only a dream.

It's still dark outside. Someone is in the room.

The light comes on. I see Tad. Thank God! I must have slept a long time.

"What's wrong?" he asks. "You're crying."

"It's nothing," I say, unable to repeat the dream.

He hands me an envelope.

"Look inside," he says softly.

I can feel the hard shape of my passport inside the envelope.

"I reminded the official of his escapade and he decided to co-operate. I saved him once before from another disgrace. He owed me this one. That's how I got your passport back."

I gather my belongings, but something is tugging at my heart. I feel the weight of the gold locket on my chest. An idea takes flight. I can't leave Teresa like this. I must establish a link between us, whatever the outcome.

"Tad, can we stop by the convent?"

"Slava, you are mad. At a time like this! Why?"

I tell him.

He shakes his head and looks at me as if I were crazy.

We get in the car. It's dawn. Everything around us is bathed in blue light. I am squeezing the gold locket tightly inside a clenched fist. We speed down the road. There is no one behind us.

We arrive in Kolkov. Tad stops in front of the convent. I get out and ring the bell, praying for Sister Ursula to appear. In a moment a black and white ball rolls out of the convent's door. It's her!

I hand her the locket and beg her to give it discreetly to Teresa.

She hesitates at first, then agrees and slips it into the pocket of her habit. Sister Ursula understands without too many words. We hug and say goodbye.

Tad and I are speeding toward the airport. I'm in tears. I have just parted with a treasure I received from my dearest grandma. On the other hand, I still have the Pushkin book. Even if Teresa isn't my sister, I've given something of value in my sister's name to a lost Jewish child.

"You did right, Slava," says Tad. "You did right."

We arrive at the airport.

Tad takes me all the way to the plane. He shows my documents to different officers, who scan me as if I were an escaped convict under extradition orders.

Throughout this protocol and red tape, I am constantly aware of Tad's warmth and caring, and of the inevitable moment of parting that hangs over us.

It's time to board the plane.

My feet don't want to move. There are people milling about, but I don't care. We cling to each other like two children. Tad puts something into my coat pocket and takes my arm, guiding me onto the first step.

At the top, I turn around to wave to him. He waves back. There are tears in his eyes.

I walk inside and sit down. I cannot see him from my seat. Soon the plane begins to taxi for takeoff. While I am sorry to leave Tad, I feel relieved to be leaving Poland.

My seat is next to the window, but I can't see anything. It's as if now, when it's finally safe to fall apart, I want to cry and cry. But tears don't come. Only thoughts of all that's happened go round and round.

The plane lifts off. I see Warsaw fade below layers of greyness and with it Babushka, Basia, and Teresa. I think of poor Zofia. Those are all good people who will live in my memories forever.

Tad is very vivid in my mind. I pull the small package out of my pocket. It is wrapped in rough tissue, like the toilet paper you find in Polish toilets, if you are lucky. I tear open the tissue and find a silver medallion with a Polish eagle on it. How could he have known that I would give up my locket? Tad was uncanny! On the other side of the medallion is an engraved message:

WITH ALL MY TRUEST AND IMPOSSIBLE LOVE
THE SKYLARK

Inside the medallion, behind glass, is his photograph. Also enclosed in toilet tissue is a wrinkled ten-pound note.

It'll come in handy in London.

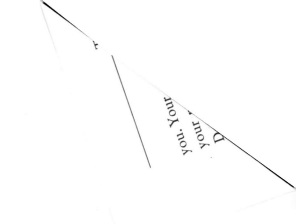
you. Your
your. D

Off Again

19

It is a week later, and I am up in a plane again, burrowing a path in the sky to Montreal and Miriam's wedding. I've left Tadeusz in Poland, Dorothea and Mur in London. My thoughts won't leave them, though the events of the past few weeks now seem a distant and almost fantastic tale. Staring into the light-infused clouds, I conjure up the faces of my dear friends and relive the events of my last days in London with Dorothea and Mur.

On arriving in London, I realized that the ten-pound note Tadeusz gave me was practically the only money I had left in the world. I used some of it to take a taxi to Dorothea's house, praying that she would be there when I arrived.

I rang the bell. The door opened, and there she was, standing behind her maid.

"Oh, Liz," she said, putting her arms around me. "I've missed you. I've been worried. There was no word from cousins telephoned that they have letters from parents and Miriam. What happened? Tell me." Dorothea sounded anxious.

"I'll tell you everything," I promised, feeling drained. It's as if everything I had experienced in the past few weeks has suddenly caught up to me here.

"Sit down. Lizzie will bring tea," urged Dorothea.

Even in my weakened state, I had to chuckle. "You English think tea is a cure for all that ails you."

Dorothea laughed. "It's a whole lot better than pills."

Soon Lizzie brought in tea, biscuits, sandwiches, and a chocolate torte. I ate as if this were my last meal on earth. Maybe there *was* something magically medicinal about the ritual of tea, I concluded, beginning to feel energized. Slowly, I proceeded to tell Dorothea all about Poland.

She listened for a long time without interrupting.

"It's hard to believe that you went through all that!" she exclaimed, incredulity in her voice. "I live such a sheltered life compared to you."

I handed her the gift I had chosen for her while passing a folk-art shop in Warsaw. A white-fringed shawl with vermilion roses and green leaves scattered all over it. She threw it over her shoulders, and looked like a beautiful Polish princess playing a country girl.

She bid me go upstairs, wash up and change my clothes. The plush-blue bedroom was pacifying after the muddy greyness of the Polish hotel, the prison cell, and the room in the country. *Blue Boy* stared calmly at me out of his portrait above the bed, ageless and unaffected by the frenzy of life around him.

I telephoned Mur, who was not at home, also Max's cousins, who were.

Lola sounded relieved on the phone. "You've been away for ages. I've had a letter from your mother, who is quite worried about you. Please come for lunch tomorrow, Slava, and bring your friend."

I agreed.

The next day Dorothea and I set out for lunch at Max's cousins'. Lola asked a million questions about our "trip."

"But Dorothea was home already last week when I called, and you weren't." Lola sounded puzzled. I could not possibly tell her the whole truth, as the news would immediately make its way to Mama and Max.

"I only came home for two days to see my parents, while Slava stayed behind," chirped up loyal Dorothea.

Lola had a look of resignation on her face, but seemed satisfied by this.

I opened and read the two letters waiting for me. One from Mama with the usual questions, warnings, and pleadings. I promised myself I would write to her as soon as I got back to Dorothea's.

Miriam's letter bubbled with anticipation about her forthcoming wedding. She can't wait to see me, and hopes that the dress turned out well. Please bring the bill and remember the dress is on her.

We stayed at Lola's until well after lunch, then said our goodbyes and went to the dressmaker's.

The dress was ready. It was cornflower blue, full-skirted, with a tiny bodice, low neckline, and short, puffy sleeves.

"You look beautiful!" exclaimed Dorothea, looking at me with admiration. The dress fit perfectly. The dressmaker placed it in a box. "How much?" I asked, worried about the money I owed.

"The dress is a gift from me," answered Dorothea.

Good, kind, sweet Dorothea! I couldn't thank her enough. Although Miriam had wanted to reimburse me for the dress, I didn't have the money to pay for it now, so Dorothea's gift was very timely.

When we got home, I called Mur again. This time he answered. I detected a huge relief in his voice when he heard mine. He came over immediately. Dorothea left us alone to talk.

"I've been worried about you," said Mur, greeting me warmly. "That was a nasty thing that happened to us. Tad saved us both from what could have been a tragic end."

I couldn't agree more. After all that happened, Tad really came through for me.

"On a happier note," said Mur, "I have two cheques here for you. Your honorarium, as promised, and an advance on the next lot of translations."

"But it won't be for a while," I warned him, "because I am going to Montreal first."

"That's OK," he said kindly, "whenever you can do them."

Three days passed since my return from Warsaw. Dorothea took me to her hairdresser, who trimmed and curled my hair. I must admit, I looked quite glamorous.

A few days later, Mur and Dorothea took me to the airport. More goodbyes, I thought sadly. We vowed to meet again soon. As I was leaving, Mur handed me a letter from Tad, which I slipped into my purse to read on the plane.

"Here is my address in Montreal, should you need to get in touch. I'll be there for at least ten days," I told them. I couldn't bear to lose contact with either one.

I clung to Mur, feeling deep friendship and love for this man who had so much reminded me of Papa. I kissed Dorothea, who handed me a small package.

While waiting for the plane to lift off, I opened Dorothea's gift. It was a red leather wallet stuffed with money. The note said:

> My sweet friend, here are some Canadian dollars I had left over from my stay at the school in Victoria. I want you to have them. I love you dearly and I'll miss you awfully.
>
> As always
Dorothea

There were about five hundred dollars in Canadian money! Dorothea must have guessed that I really needed it. I vowed to repay her as soon as I got home and cashed my cheques.

I pulled Tad's letter from my purse and began to read.

> Dearest Slava,
>
> Please don't feel lonely. My thoughts are with you. I promise again to do what I had promised earlier. I'll work on your case as it is all I have left of you now.
>
> I apologize for having stolen a part of your father's file. The photographs of Mortynski and your father,

the picture of Basia, and the court case between M. and your father. Forgive me, but I need them if I am to keep my promise.

Whatever you do with your life, for heaven's sake do it right! Don't keep on running away from love. Look who is talking. I still do it. But though I am not a romantic I want to quote something I remember from a book I read. An old woman says to a younger man:

"There are many bad criminals, but the worst of all is the one who murders love."

I know all about this.

All my love
Your faithful and devoted friend
Tadeusz

I looked into the leather pouch and noticed how thin the file was. I giggled to myself when I thought of what a sweet scoundrel Tadeusz proved to be to the very end.

The woman sitting next to me on the plane gives me a perturbed look. I guess she thinks I must be a crazy young girl, to be talking and laughing to myself as I reread the letters from my friends. She leans over to the man across the aisle. "Elle est folle!" she exclaims, assuming I don't understand French. I giggle to myself. No wonder French is being spoken here. We are, after all, on our way to Montreal!

Perhaps, I conclude, as drowsiness sets in with the hypnotic buzz of the airplane engines, my strange life is turning me into *une femme folle!*

On an airplane, everything goes topsy-turvy as you

travel through different time zones. Hours pass and a day is lost as the plane nears Montreal. Faces of Dorothea, Mur and Tad fade somewhat, while the faces of Miriam and Joshua become sharper. I know now that what I had experienced with Tadeusz was a romantic love, the kind that people say doesn't last. Strange that my feelings for Joshua are still there, though I can't define them.

And Adam? His features remain vague.

Montreal, Mon Amour!

I rescue my luggage at Customs, and walk into a waiting room full of people.

Montreal's charm is its people. The French Canadians give this city a distinct character of lightness. Although I have not been to Paris I sense a European ambience here, even at the airport. From my mother's descriptions of Warsaw before the war, this atmosphere is similar. The lively language, the warm manner of greeting, the bistros, the pervasive smell of coffee.

"Polachka!" someone calls.

"Miriam!"

We embrace as if nothing had happened. As if there had been no betrayal. As if Miriam had not fallen in love with Joshua and gone off with him into the pinky-beige romance of the Israeli desert.

Some of the old pain returns momentarily, but there is no time for self-pity.

Miriam chirps happily away about the wedding, her

love for her groom, and having me here. She sounds as though she means every word.

How do I feel? A little strange, but glad I had the courage to come.

Sitting next to Miriam, listening to her chatter, I observe the streets. For some inexplicable reason, I feel Papa's presence in the wide sidewalks we walked together, the store windows we admired, and the cafés we frequented. This city is the last link with my past and my childhood.

"Hey, Polachka, you're off and dreaming!" Miriam has not lost her exuberance. I slip quickly forward, into the present.

"Before we go home, let's stop here for coffee. There just happens to be a parking place." Miriam backs the car into the space with one try.

It is three o'clock in the afternoon on St. Lawrence Street. There are several tables outside a deli. The Deli! The one Papa had bought back in 1947, where Miriam and I had worked so hard. It's still here, and it's busy.

People are still lining up for herring, salami, corned beef, and pickles. Not to mention bagels! As before when I worked here, transactions are being made in three languages: Yiddish, English, and French. There are different people working here now, older ones. They carry out their customers' orders with a kind of bored expertise. There is none of the ingénue-type of service that we young girls and my inexperienced father-lawyer turned deli-operator had provided.

Orders fly about, landing inside the brown paper bags.

Miriam orders two coffees and cheese Danishes. Yum.

We carry our goodies to a table spotted with dried-up puddles of chocolate milk. After wiping the surface with a wet napkin, Miriam puts the tray down, and we settle into the rickety bridge chairs.

The Danish is plump with sweet cheese, yellow with egg yolks, and tart with lemons.

In front of us is a fruit and vegetable market under an open sky. Carts full of produce pass by, pulled by horses. Balls of brown horse dung plop onto the road.

"Joshua wants to see you," says Miriam carefully.

The thing I most dread! Meeting with Joshua after all this time. I've carried this image with me for almost three years. How will I be able to face him after what had happened between the three of us?

"When?" I inquire, with a mouth full of Danish.

"Whenever you say. Tonight."

"So soon? I am not ready."

"Look, Polachka," says Miriam with that decisive and self-assured manner I have always envied. "I know how you must feel. About me. About Josh. But time has passed. You need to face your demons. Why not get it over with?"

What Miriam doesn't realize is that I feel strange even with her. The pain and anguish they caused me with their little jaunt together. Can it ever be completely forgiven and forgotten? How could I ever trust them again?

Forgiveness came to me much more easily at a distance. As for a face-to-face with Joshua, perhaps I should get it over with.

I shrug my shoulders, feigning indifference, and say yes. I feel trapped but won't make waves just before Miriam's wedding.

On the way to Miriam's home, we pass through Westmount. I find myself on a familiar street. We pass number 50 Academy Road. We lived there as a family. I capture a memory like an eagle its prey.

The balcony on the second floor where we sat on scorching summer nights. The bedroom window through which I could hear Papa's cries of pain as I arrived home from school. The living room with its black ceiling.

The playground across which I walked home from school with a boy, afraid that Papa would see us through the window and punish me. One day he did.

"What were you two doing?" he asked suspiciously after I came home.

"We were only walking, Papa!" I answered, fearfully.

He stared at me angrily, and slapped my face for the first time ever.

Then he clutched his side as his face twisted with pain.

Later, he'd wanted to make up by inviting me out for ice cream.

"Our good old school," announces Miriam.

A block down the street stands the old Westmount Junior High where, at Friday night dances, I grew from a wallflower into a pretty good dancer.

"This is where Mike and I are going to live after the wedding," says Miriam excitedly, driving further down the street. "The third balcony from the ground," she points. "See?"

I wish her a big mazel tov.

We then drive to her parents' home in the Jewish section of Montreal.

There are still barrels of dill pickles standing outside the small grocery stores. The air is still pleasingly scented with freshly baked bread.

The Silvermans, Miriam's parents, are happy to see me. They show me into the small bedroom upstairs, which I am to make my home for ten days. I used to stay here when Miriam invited me for a sleepover. Those were a riot, all-night marathons of listening to music and talking.

I present Miriam with her gift: a Polish shawl similar in style to the white one I gave Dorothea, only Miriam's shawl has golden roses on a black background.

Finally, alone in my room, I feel more relaxed. It's not the same as it used to be with Miriam, when we were both innocent and free-spirited. Now there are heavier issues in our lives. We have entered adulthood.

There is noise out in the hall. A door opens and closes, then I hear voices. Obviously, the guests have arrived.

Someone knocks on my door.

"Come in," I say, displeased to have so little time to myself.

Miriam pokes in her head. "It's time for dinner, Polachka. Mama wants you at the table."

I comb my hair, change into the dress Tad and Mur had bought me in London, and put on some lipstick. The mirror reflects a pretty image.

The dinner guests are already seated. As I walk in, Miriam introduces me to Mike, her husband-to-be. A nice-looking, tall, red-haired, blue-eyed man. I see a familiar back. I proceed to my chair and face Joshua, who is seated across from me.

21
Joshua

Joshua has changed. He now wears a crewcut. His face no longer has a young boy look, though he is only twenty-one. His eyes have retained that same light I had seen there three long years ago. I wonder what he is thinking about me.

At the table, we exchange dumb hellos and how-are-yous. These meaningless social niceties when no one is even listening to the answers. It's awkward, and all I can do to hold my own is chew on a piece of challah or turn to my neighbour, Miriam's dad, who is saying words I am not registering. I have never been good at small talk.

The host pours some sweet kosher wine.

I gulp it down like ginger ale, conscious of Joshua's constant stare.

"I hear you've just arrived from London," he says at last, his dark eyes fixed on me.

"Yes, I was invited to go there," I explain dryly, "because I'd written some English translations of a Polish poet's work." I struggle for the right words, trying to sound grown up and important, but in reality I feel more like a frightened kid with a pounding heart.

"That's great! You were always creative. But to translate poetry? You'd have to be a poet. And you are."

Joshua always knew the right thing to say.

Chicken soup with matzo balls is served. Miriam observes me intently. Every so often she whispers something to Mike. They seem very much love, holding hands under the table. More red wine is poured into my cup. I observe it as it seeps into my glass and remember Tad: that evening in London and afterwards at the Polish country house. Those times now seem like a vivid dream that fades with the onset of morning.

"What about you?" I finally manage to ask Joshua, wine warming my temples.

"I'm going to the University of Montreal. Studying engineering."

I don't comment. I know nothing about engineering. In fact I now know very little about Joshua. Thankfully, the conversation shifts to Miriam's mom and dad and the wedding.

I struggle through the courses of brisket and carrot tzimis, then dessert. One more minute of this artificial situation, and I might choke on the angel food cake. It tastes like cotton batting, until the chocolate sauce comes around. That is soothing.

By the end of dinner, I feel giddy, having drunk so much wine.

After the meal, we are invited into the living room. The

floor feels unsteady under my feet as I make my way there, swaying like the stem of a wilting flower. I trip over a footstool. Joshua comes around to steady me. Naturally, I think dazedly, that's the real Joshua, gallant as always. Do I detect mockery in those eyes? Or is it my own mockery? He seems taller than before, even with my two-inch high-heeled shoes. His hand feels warm and strong on my shoulder. An old feeling creeps in, and my wine-diluted mind feels panicky. No, please, not that again.

Miriam's mom hands me a letter from home. I put it in my pocket to read later.

We sit around for a while and chat about the logistics of the wedding. Joshua is the best man. That means that I will have to walk in and out of the chapel with him.

They discuss the bridal dinner, to be held tomorrow, after a rehearsal at the synagogue.

I am beginning to feel slightly nauseated.

Miriam senses something is wrong, and takes me into another room, where a table is laid with wedding gifts.

"Sit here," she says and disappears. A moment later she returns with a glass full of fizz. "Drink," she commands, as Miriam can. I drink it to the bottom. The cold fizzy liquid goes down well. In a little while I feel a bit better.

"I didn't get you a gift yet," I say, holding my splitting head between my hands.

"Take these," says Miriam, handing me two Aspirins. I swallow them with difficulty. I sense someone standing over my chair, next to Miriam. I look up at them. Joshua and Miriam, my best friends. They make a cute couple, I think derisively.

"Weren't we supposed to meet in Jerusalem near your kibbutz after you two eloped?" I ask, oozing sarcasm. How could I have said that now, with Mike standing nearby?

There is an awful silence. It's time for me, I think giddily, after all I've been through, to embarrass somebody else for a change.

But I know this thinking is wrong, only I can't seem to help myself.

"I have a day off tomorrow; would you like me to take you shopping?" says Joshua, breaking the icy spell. Why does he have to be here to see me in my alcoholic state?

"Yes, that would be nice," I say weakly, swallowing my words, desperate to go upstairs and lie down. Soon my wishes come true, and I hear people leaving. Joshua kisses me on the cheek.

"Pick you up at ten," he says.

"Yes, good night," I respond and crawl upstairs, belching gas from the seltzer. I flop into bed, admitting to myself that spending time alone with Joshua is something I really want to do.

Unable to fall asleep, I toss, then read the letter from home. Mama writes that I am to telegram her as soon as I get to Montreal. She misses me and it's time I came home. I've been away too long and she is worried.

The thought of going home depresses me. There is nothing in Vancouver I want to do except see Mama and Pyza. And I am more confused than ever about Adam.

For some reason, I look inside the empty envelope before putting Mama's letter in it. There's a tiny piece of

paper folded into a flat roll. It's a note from Adam.
He writes:

Dear Elizabeth,

It's been ages since I have heard from you. I'm sure
you found more interesting things to do in Europe
than writing letters to us back here in Vancouver. I
missed you a lot and I'd like to know if you missed me
at all. Your mother tells me that you're in Montreal
for a week or two. What a coincidence! I am travelling
to Quebec City next week and will be dropping into
Montreal around the 9th of August. I have your friend
Miriam's telephone number, and hope I can call you
and maybe get to see you.

> All the best
> Love
> *Adam*

Oh, no! Not Adam too! He would have to worm his way
into the wedding. Why did Mama have to remind him?
Trying to dismiss my gassy stomach and aching head, I
run next door to Miriam, just as I used to before I left
Montreal for good. I tell her the terrible news about
Adam!

"Don't you like Adam?" responds Miriam, without
empathy. "I mean, he's your boyfriend after all. There is
nothing you can do about it now. Of course Adam is invited to the wedding if he wishes to come. But what about
Josh?"

I am too exhausted to think now. "As Scarlett O'Hara
says," I tell Miriam, "in *Gone With The Wind*, 'I won't
think about it now. Tomorrow is another day'."

Miriam laughs. "Something like that. You've still got your sense of humour."

The barrier between us is beginning to crumble. We sit on the bed and talk into the night. Just like old times. I apologize for my after-dinner remarks. Miriam nods silently in acknowledgement.

When I eventually sleep, I dream that I have lost my way in Warsaw.

I'm running away! Down millions and millions of stairs. Unending stairs, and at the bottom there are bars. Mortynski and Tad are on the other side, laughing at me. I can't get out of here, ever!

I wake up wondering for a moment whether the whole Warsaw caper really happened. Will anyone believe me when I tell them about it? I decide to keep it to myself for the time being.

Today is the ninth of August, and Adam is arriving some time later. In the meantime, I've got to get dressed and be ready for Joshua.

He comes right on time, dressed casually in cotton pants and a checkered shirt. I am in my old blue dress and sandals.

"I was able to get my uncle's car," he says with a happy grin.

In the front seat of the huge Oldsmobile, I can't help but think back to the old days when we simply took the streetcar. Everything seems so different now, except the old feeling of warmth I still feel for Josh.

We drive downtown, park the car, and go into a department store. The huge array of things in the china department makes me dizzy. A pair of beautiful sterling silver candlesticks catches my eye, but the price is more than I can afford. The sales clerk sees my hesitation. "We have the same thing in silver plate," she says. Those are as beautiful but heavier. The price is right. I tell her to gift-wrap them.

That done, we decide to have lunch at the restaurant upstairs.

"It's my treat," offers Joshua.

I accept and we sit down.

An awkward moment of silence passes between us. I can't stand it anymore.

"You and Miriam hurt me. Why?" I blurt out the inevitable, feeling like an idiot, unable to eat my cottage cheese and fruit salad.

Joshua looks down at his sandwich.

"We were wrong," he answers simply. "I could give you a number of reasons, but they wouldn't excuse the wrong."

I am surprised and taken aback that he would admit it.

"Is that all you have to say?" I prod mercilessly.

"Yes," he replies, "except that I think I still love you."

He thinks he still loves me? I nibble at my food, not sure of anything.

No more is said. Joshua takes me home and we part on a lukewarm note.

Miriam's mother gives me a message from Adam. He is in town and he'll call back.

I don't feel like seeing him. I feel selfish. I just want to straighten things out with Joshua, without Adam. Mrs.

Silverman gives me a questioning look as I stand there, forgetting her presence. I explain that Adam is a friend from Vancouver.

Ten minutes later the phone rings.

"Hi, Liz, how are you?"

"I'm fine thanks, how are you?" I lie, feeling agitated and unable to think of anything nice to say. We make arrangements to meet at the Temple later, where the rehearsal is being held. I give him the address while agonizing about what I am going to do with both him and Joshua there.

An hour later, Miriam returns from the beauty parlour.

"Look, Polachka. He is here. There is nothing you can do. I know you still love Josh and he loves you. But neither of you are going to admit it. Let Adam solve the problem."

"What do you mean?" I ask, puzzled. Miriam was always more practical than I was, and more cunning socially. I never could understand the games people played.

"When you see them together, you'll know."

"Maybe I don't want either one." I sound cynical.

"It's your life, babe," answers the old-for-her-age, wise Miriam.

I dress for the evening with huge doubts about my life. I dawdle with my hair while they shout "hurry up" from downstairs.

We arrive at the chapel a few minutes late. The rest of the wedding party is already waiting. We are just starting to practise our walk down the aisle, my arm through Joshua's, when Adam enters the chapel.

He comes over and puts his arm around me posses-
sively while I introduce him to Joshua.

I glance sideways at Joshua to catch his reaction, but
the look on his face is inscrutable.

Adam sits down in the front pew and watches as Joshua
and I parade up and down the aisle half-a-dozen times,
arm in arm.

Adam

"I've missed you," says Adam the next day, at lunch. "Here, take this." He hands me a velvet box.

I open the box reluctantly, and find his fraternity pin nestling in white satin lining. This is serious. When a boy gives a girl his frat pin, it means they're almost engaged.

Ambivalence surges through me. I do like Adam. He is steady, consistent, and seems devoted to me. He can also be critical and self-serving. How could I possibly accept his pin now, when I am trying to work out my feelings for Joshua?

"Adam," I say, feeling guilty and awkward. "I can't accept this. I am confused about things between us and I don't even know if I want to go back to Vancouver."

Adam's face reddens. His eyes grow large and moist. He takes the box off the table and puts it in his pocket. He is hurt.

"I suspected something was wrong here. You obviously care nothing for me."

I twist my paper napkin into shreds. The truth wavering on the edge of my tongue.

I can't tell him about Joshua after all this time, or even mention Tadeusz. Would it help him to know this, no matter how painful? But isn't it worse, when you're hurt, to suffer in the dark without knowing why?

"Adam, there is something you don't know."

I tell him the whole story from the beginning. I tell him about Joshua but hold back about Tadeusz and Warsaw, until I have first told Mama and Max.

"Why did you keep all this secret?" he asks angrily. "You led me on and on. What kind of person are you?"

I explain my inability to talk about myself. How at St. Anne's I even lied about being Jewish.

"How could you have lied about being Jewish? You're dishonest, Elizabeth, and act like a coward!" exclaims Adam.

"You were the one always telling me to forget my past. Well, Joshua was a big part of it," I cry out, hurt at his accusations.

I become daring and tell him about Tadeusz and our friendship.

Adam grimaces as if he were seeing an apparition. His fingers thump against the table.

"You have changed Elizabeth. Into what, though?"

I can't answer. Maybe he is right. I feel so ashamed.

"It's either him or me. You have one day to make up your mind." Adam's chin has that stubborn look to it. He drops me off at the streetcar and promptly walks away with his hands in his pockets. I guess he must feel what I felt when I discovered Joshua was going away with Miriam.

The meeting with Adam leaves me depressed. On the way home my head begins to ache. When I finally get there, Miriam hands me a special delivery letter from England. It's from Andrzej Mur.

I tear it open and read.

My Dear Slava,

Here's a note from Tad. He managed to pass it on to me through a friend. Miss you.

> Be well
> *Andrzej*

I tear open the letter from Tad.

Dearest Slava,

I hope that Mur passes this on to you. I have also sent him the rest of your file via messenger. I am certain he will mail it on to you.

I want to tell you briefly what transpired after you left. I was able to get M. held for questioning. The Richtmans' letter helped to make Scarface and the Official finally scratch their heads about Mortynski. It's a start. I'll let you know what happens. Mur will send the next letter to your Vancouver address.

I have visited Teresa. She is a very lonely child. I told her you will write to her from Canada.

I missed "us" after you left. Marysia has become a sympathetic companion. I know, and you know, that you and I had no future together other than friendship. Keep writing and translating. Never stop. I hope that you too will find your true soulmate sometime, somewhere. Please don't feel lonely and alone.

I will always love you in my own way.

Skylark

It dawns on me that the loneliness and aloneness Tad speaks of is something I have always done my best to hide, even from myself.

Now, I think of little Teresa in a dreary convent struggling with the same thing. Does she long for someone to share her thoughts and feelings with, like I do? Someone who understands her past and her present? Someone who wouldn't criticize or constantly place blame? I feel deep inside that she will not become a nun and remain alone for the rest of her life.

After long deliberation, I decide that the person whose friendship and understanding I need and long for is definitely not Adam.

I call up all the courage and emotional energy I have left, and telephone him at his hotel.

He comes over and we go for a walk. "I cannot choose now, nor can I promise anything," I say. "I am terribly sorry to have hurt you."

"You're hurting yourself, Elizabeth," he replies sadly. "Don't you long for security, a home and children? I could give you all that and more."

"Children? Of course I want them someday. But not for a long time. They need care and love. I am not capable of that. Not yet, Adam."

Of course I want security and a home, I speak silently to myself. I hate being dependent on my parents. But

I have to be honest. A marriage and a husband seem a labyrinth of problems to take on, topping ones I already have.

"Besides, I don't think I am in love with you, Adam," I say simply.

He nods, looking downcast.

We say goodbye, looking at each other like players who have just lost a game.

If Mama and Max only knew what I've just done!

The next day, there's a frantic phone call from Mama. She's found out. Adam called to tell his mother, who called Mama. Mama cries into the receiver, and Max shouts on another line. They've had it with me. "Come home immediately. Do you hear?" are their last threatening words. I respond in a hard and rebellious manner.

I am not going to oblige them until well after the wedding.

The Wedding Bouquet

The circle is almost complete. I am flying to Vancouver on a small, noisy plane with a million stops. In lifting upwards, you relinquish the earth. You hang adrift in the nowhere land whose intangible quality invites the past as the only sure point of connection with life. My mental diary flips through the pages of all that has happened so far. Miriam's wedding has been a turning point in my life.

August the eleventh, the wedding day finally arrived like a messenger bearing gifts and flowers of joy.

Here I was again, preening myself in the mirror that reflected an image of a blond-haired young woman in blue. Soon we were to meet outside in the park for pictures, then drive on to the temple for the wedding ceremony. The reception was to take place in the grand hall next door.

Satisfied with my image in the mirror, I went to the window and looked out at the tall trees, trying to collect my thoughts. I remembered how at St. Anne's I talked to a maple tree as if it were my friend. Good old Mapleton. I would confide in it as I did in the Sunflower Diary, all my innermost thoughts. I closed my eyes and remembered the tree's green rustling arms and silky leaves reaching in through the window. Isn't it strange how certain images remain in one's mind forever? It is no different than an album of photographs. Just a simple image of old Mapleton pacified me and enabled me to continue on my road through this day.

Outside in the foyer stood a crystal bowl of orange juice and champagne. I helped myself, and, having gulped it down, went to Miriam's room.

She was also standing in front of the mirror. The long gown embossed with lacy flowers adorned her slim body as a cherry blossom adorns a tree.

Her dark hair was pinned up and topped with a tiara of tiny fresh stephanotis, holding up a fingertip veil of tulle.

I handed her my other gift: pearl earrings.

"Here is for something new," I said.

"And here's for something old, from Mama," she laughed, lifting up her gown to show me a blue garter above her knee.

Miriam was ravishing in her wedding attire. Happiness shone in her face like a sun rising in the morning sky. It was enviable to see, but I didn't feel envious. All the differences that may have arisen between us once, I put aside to wish my friend the best that life can offer.

We hugged, our eyes full of happy tears. When we pulled apart, our only concern was smudged mascara.

The photographer was waiting in the park across the street from the apartment building.

The parents of the groom had just arrived. The florist delivered the bouquets and corsages.

Miriam's bouquet was of white orchids and sprays of stephanotis.

Mine was pink roses and baby's breath.

The groom and best man arrived. Joshua looked princely in his white tuxedo jacket and black pants. His boutonniere was a single red carnation.

We posed for pictures. It was a tedious procedure as the heels of my new shoes kept sinking into the grass. After dozens of poses, the groom and best man left, taking me with them. Miriam rode with her mother and father, who tooted the horn all the way to the temple.

People were gathering outside. The ladies wore dresses of sequins, silk, and satin in all shades of flowers and rainbows. The gentlemen were more subdued, in dark suits, white shirts, and ties.

Mike's friends were ushering the ladies to their seats. And the gentlemen wore white yarmulkes with the letters M&M inscribed in gold.

The atmosphere was solemn among the blue velvet pews, stained windows, and brilliant chandeliers. A pungent smell of roast chicken wafted in from the reception hall.

We lined up at the door. Miriam's uncle began to sing "Till The End of Time." This was our cue.

First the groom. Then the best man with Miriam's mother. Then it was my turn. As I walked slowly down the aisle I noted that the guests wore that "weddingy" look of excitement mixed with admiration. Then I went up under the canopy, on the bride's side. Joshua stood opposite me.

The music stopped. Miriam and her father appeared in the doorway. Everyone stood up and the wedding march began to play. Miriam, sparkling with happiness, walked down the aisle on her father's arm. When they got to the canopy, her father gave her to Mike. The ceremony began with the usual vows, and Joshua presented the groom with the ring. I had to lift Miriam's veil so she could sip the wine, and I practically fell over her mother.

A cup was placed under Mike's foot. When he stepped on it, you could hear a crash and the crowd murmured, "Mazel tov." Prayers and chants by the cantor followed. Miriam was in tears. I found myself staring at Joshua, imagining what it would be like if this were happening to us.

The married couple went to sign the register while everyone waited. Afterwards they emerged and led our small procession out of the temple. As we walked together, I felt Joshua's arm tighten around mine.

We walked to the reception hall, where people were beginning to line up for drinks, and the hors d'oeuvres— miniature knishes—were being passed around.

A buffet table was sumptuously laid with fine silverware, white china, and crystal glasses. There were flowers, and candles, and platters of roast chicken and brisket.

Conversations were fragmented, with so many trying to chat with each other. This was difficult particularly at the buffet table. The line never seemed to move. People stood over the food, filling their plates to the brim. Then they talked while they ate, their mouths filled with delectables, which they spat out together with their words. My dress was beginning to carry the full menu of meats and salads. On occasion I had to wipe off food bits that landed on my face.

Miriam was the fairy queen of the night. I didn't do so badly either, enjoying the company of admirers gathering around me. Joshua stood on the side, alone, sipping wine.

Dessert was a chocolate skyscraper cake decorated with marzipan strawberries. A miniature marzipan couple graced the top of the cake. There was a special home-baking table. Throngs of people gathered around it, piling dozens of cakes onto their plates to take back to their tables. I found it almost impossible to get near the sweets. I pushed in with the rest, listening to many complain that they were on a diet but couldn't resist the chocolate morsels.

After dinner, the orchestra gathered on the stage and started playing. Miriam and Mike, Miriam's parents, and Joshua and I were the first couples on the dance floor for the anniversary waltz. Soon everyone joined us—small children and many other combinations of partners. The horas followed, and all the single women, young and old, thin and plump, whooped it up, shimmying and bouncing up and down and sideways.

Joshua and I danced non-stop. This was the first time we had been this close since I left Montreal.

We were both perspiring from frenzied jitterbugging.

"Let's take a walk outside," he said, wiping his forehead with a hankie.

Outside it was dark and hot. There was a small garden with a bench at the side of the temple. It was wonderful to be away from the crowd.

"What happened to Adam?" asked Joshua.

"He left for Vancouver."

"Aren't you running again, Liz?"

I shook my head "no," and thought back to that night three years ago when I ran out of Miriam's party, thinking that Joshua liked another girl. I was wrong then. But this was different. Joshua and I had an old score to settle before I could get on with my life.

"So, what is happening with you?" He placed the emphasis on "is."

I told him the truth about Adam.

He didn't answer, only took my hand and held it.

We both knew that it was time to return to the party.

Miriam was standing up on a chair, ready to throw her wedding bouquet into the crowd.

I ran into the middle of the throng. The bouquet flew through the air and plummeted down straight into my arms.

"You're next," someone shouted.

I looked around for Joshua but he had disappeared. When I began to dance with other guests, I saw him with a pretty dark-haired girl. They danced together for the rest of the evening. I felt jealous and uncomfortable. After Miriam and Mike left, people began to disperse. Joshua came over and offered to take me home. I accepted without making a fuss over his dancing partner, though I wanted to ask him about her.

We drove to the Silvermans' in silence. At the door, he kissed me on the cheek and handed me my two bouquets of flowers, which I had left in the back seat of the car.

"When are you leaving?" he asked.

"In two days. But I have to visit my father's grave before I leave Montreal."

"So soon?" Joshua sounded sad. "I'll take you there tomorrow," he offered.

I was grateful, though I dreaded it. I had not been to the cemetery since I last left Montreal, and that seemed like a long time ago.

"Tomorrow at two?"

I agreed and went inside, into my bedroom. I sat down on the bed, too exhausted to turn on the light. There was no one in the room next door. Miriam was married. Joshua was ambivalent. I was at loose ends.

In the centre of my chest I felt a void, surrounded by a wall. Loneliness crept into it like an uninvited guest.

The next day passed slowly. I tried to pack, but felt too lethargic, so gave it up after a while. I was due to leave tomorrow.

When Joshua came I was ready, sombrely dressed in beige and black. We were already at the door when he suggested I take my bridal bouquet of roses to the grave.

I had not thought of it. Nor had I written a note to Papa to leave on his tombstone, which I often used to do.

My mood was drab as we approached the Baron de Hirsch Cemetery. I took a little map of the cemetery out of my purse. We walked through the gates onto the grounds filled with grey and black stones of different sizes. Here and there were flowers placed at gravesides. Here and there were dug graves as yet unfilled.

We walked a long way to the place where I thought Papa was buried, but we couldn't find the tombstone. I'd been here so many times. It was as if I didn't want to find it! Even the map wasn't much help.

Eventually we separated. Joshua looked on one side while I looked on the other. How did I ever find it before? Could it have disappeared?

The strong sunlight pounded my head and blinded my eyes. It was hot and dry here, like a desert. I became frantic. I walked and ran, stepping all over other people's graves. Half-crazed from the heat and the futile search, I was ready to fall onto the ground from sheer exhaustion when I heard Joshua's voice.

"I found it! I found it!"

I went to where he stood. His forehead was drenched. His shirt had huge wet marks on it. But he was smiling as he handed me the flowers, which he had carefully wrapped in wet newspaper. That was Joshua!

The tombstone was totally different from the one I remembered visiting before I left Montreal for Vancouver. Then it seemed larger, and the black granite more lustrous, garlanded with multicoloured flowers. This one was smaller, grey with dust and flanked by weeds. It said nothing to me about Papa. The pink rose bouquet looked startlingly alive next to this faded granite marker of Papa's final resting place.

I stood there for a long time remembering life.

My life with Papa. His goodness and honesty. How he worked to save us from the Nazis. The effects of the genocide on all our lives.

I began to weep, and the tears fell onto Papa's grave. Sobs seemed to be coming from that void in my chest where loneliness lived. I stood at the graveside for a long time, remembering.

After a while my crying ceased. Something had lifted upwards and out of me, and I felt lighter and cleansed. I no longer felt the weight of the wall in my chest and the emptiness inside it. I had said my final farewell to Papa, though he would live in my heart and memory for as long as I lived.

A pair of arms wound around me. I had almost forgotten Joshua.

"Your father loved you very much," he said. "Think of all the good in your life because of him. And this love continues in the world. Maybe it just takes on a different form.

"I, too, love you," he added quickly.

I felt afraid. Afraid of love. Of losing it. Of not being worthy, and of not being able to trust anyone ever again.

In spite of these feelings, I drew strength from Joshua. Holding hands, we walked out of the cemetery into a street filled with life.

More of Life's Alterations

The plane lands at the Vancouver airport.

It's raining, as usual, and foggy. I feel nostalgic, longing to return to Montreal, to Europe, all over again.

We stand inside the stuffy plane waiting for the door to open. Vancouverites, tired, bored, returning home, and newcomers smiling, full of the adventure still ahead.

I think of the excitement I felt when leaving six weeks ago. Those weeks seem packed with a lifetime of unforgettable experience.

The line moves. I exit the plane, uncertain about how to confront Mama and Max. How to tell them about where I've been. How to make them understand that I came away from these places forever changed.

There they are. Pyza runs toward me and, as usual, excavates a hole in my cheek with a welcoming kiss. I decide to do the same and soon we're holding onto our respective cheeks, giggling. Mama's greeting is cautious. Max is looking at his watch. He is always somewhat aloof, neither displeased nor approving. I never know where I stand. Am I late or am I early?

We drive home, nostalgia on the rise. I compare the misty and unpeopled Vancouver streets with the crowded and noisy cities of London and Montreal.

If the contrast to density and noise is spaciousness and quietude, then this city wins. There is a sense of serenity here, even without the old-world charm. The mountains give this landscape a strong sense of identity. The Pacific Ocean defines this city's shores, as the little Chinese markets full of flowers and vegetables define many streets.

Back home, the ritual of dinner begins. Needless to say, all my favourite things: chicken cutlets, fried cauliflower, Polish-style gnocci, and Spanish torte. I eat the delicious food only to please Mama. My mind is so richly filled with the delectables of past events that not even my stomach requires nourishment.

After dinner I distribute the small gifts from London. Crystal salt and pepper shakers from Stratford-On-Avon for Mama. A London Bobby doll for Pyza, and a miniature Big Ben for Max.

They thank me for the gifts. Little do they know what else I have in my old brown suitcase.

I needn't have worried. Darling Pyza stands in front of us dangling my Warsaw-purchased Polish costume, with a one thousand zloty tag hanging from it.

Mama is astonished. "Where on earth did you get this, Slava?"

Max is fingering the price tag. "One thousand zloty? How much is that in dollars?"

"I got lots of zlotys for one British pound on the black market."

I've as good as told them, but they look confused.

"What black market?" wonders Max. "Where?" puzzles Mama.

"In Poland," I reply acidly, hating this interrogation. My mind feels heavy with the inevitability of the forthcoming row.

"Her friend probably bought it for her. Isn't he Polish?" Mama suggests. She is hoping, I am sure, to clear me before Max.

Max is already looking at me with accusing eyes.

Time's running out. To lie or not to lie?

How to tell them about the file and my having snooped in Max's cupboard?

"It's about Papa's file," I say very quietly, and once I start, all I want to do is get this whole thing over with as soon as possible.

I pour it all out, omitting only the parts about the prison and my brief romance with Tad. I feel entitled to some privacy.

When I finish, Mama's face is the colour of sour cream and Max's of beet borscht. In the meantime, Pyza brings in all my Polish purchases, from books to boxes.

Max stares at Mama with horror, and she at him. I have now become their demon, the evil daughter whose undesirable actions send their Edenic lives straight to hell.

Max is more afraid of Mama's reaction than of what I've done. He walks over and puts his arms around her. She sobs violently, leaning into his welcoming shoulder.

"Look what you've done to your mother!" agonizes Max.

"What I did, I did for our family. Not just for myself."

"I'll deal with you later," Max threatens hoarsely, leading Mama out of the room.

Feeling indifferent to their guilt mongering, I go to my room and play with Pyza, who knows something is up and looks at me with tearful eyes.

"Come and sit on my knee," I say, trying to pacify her. "I know I upset Mama, but all I wanted to do was find our little sister. Yours and mine."

Pyza's eyes widen.

"Our sister?" she repeats and smiles. How could a seven-year-old possibly understand about war, death and persecution, all that has led up to this moment. I'd scare her to death if I told her! But maybe I can tell her a little.

"Some time ago," I begin, "before you were born, we had a sister. She went to live with some people during the war and never returned. So, Slava went back to Poland to try to find her, but couldn't. And, because she didn't tell Mama what she had planned to do, Mama got upset."

"What's war?"

"War is when people fight one another."

"Do you and Mama have war?"

"No, silly, war is much worse. This is just a little fight."

"Slava?"

"Yes?"

"What's Poland?"

"Poland is a country where you and I and Mama and Max were born. See?" I open the old atlas that Papa gave me, and I show her Poland on the map. "That's Poland."

Pyza's eyes follow my finger past the ocean to Europe and to Poland.

"Oh," she says. She is intrigued and very serious.

Someday, when she is older, I'll tell her all about it.

Max walks into the room and sits down at my desk, turning the chair toward me. He tells Pyza to go and see Mama.

"I will not tolerate this kind of behaviour, Slava. Your mother and I have enough problems. Either you marry Adam, or go find a job and move out." Max is seething with anger. I can't listen to or look at him. My nerves are rattling my body. I can't sit still. I jump up, and walk right out of the apartment, slamming the door behind me. Now there is a war between me and him! How dare he talk to me this way!

I run around the block, again and again. It's pouring out. The usual Vancouver weather does nothing to raise my spirits. I put on a kerchief. Luckily I took my purse with me and still have a little money left in my wallet. I can't go back home, so I decide to take the bus to an old hangout of mine and Adam's, where we feasted on blueberries and ice cream. The Aristocratic on Broadway and Granville. I order a Coke. It tastes watery, so I abandon it on the counter and decide to take the bus up Granville Street.

Sitting in the back of the bus by the window, I can hardly see the street for the rain. It's getting dark and I am going nowhere. All I can think about is Joshua. The visit to Papa's grave and the plans we'd made afterwards.

After the visit to the cemetery, Josh and I went to a café for lunch.

"You can't just leave again!" he exclaimed. "Not again!"

What could I have said? I had to return to Vancouver, to face my mother. I had no other place to go. No money.

"Liz," Joshua said finally. "I have an idea! You could go to college here. I have a part-time job and could help. Now that Miriam is out of the house and her mom and dad are alone, maybe they could rent you Miriam's room in exchange for some household duties. Maybe you could teach English to immigrants in your spare time. Surely your parents would help a little, wouldn't they?"

This was the wildest idea I'd heard. I was still supposed to do translations for Mur and get money for them. It wouldn't matter where I worked on those and just maybe I could find some other part-time work.

After an hour and a half of speculation, Joshua and I came to the inevitable conclusion that I would come back to live in Montreal. I wanted that more than anything in the world. I had wanted it from the very day I left Montreal for Vancouver, three years ago.

I went home and spoke about this with Mrs. Silverman. She heard me out patiently.

"I wouldn't mind at all having you here," she said kindly. "But you are only eighteen years old and I would need your mother's permission."

"I am almost nineteen," I reminded her.

Mrs. Silverman was old-fashioned. But she was right.

I would persuade Mama when I went home that this was the best solution for all of us.

The next day Joshua and I went to a college nearby to inquire about their courses. I was able to take English and French literature as well as language courses in both languages. We even found out that the college often gave out names of good students who were willing to teach part-time. I could teach. Or, I could even work at a deli again.

I left Montreal and Joshua with sadness in my heart, but also with a twinge of hope.

Someone nudges me on the bus.

"Miss, we're at the end of the line," says the bus driver. "Here's a transfer, you can get another bus leaving here shortly. Going back," he adds pointedly.

There is a bus waiting. I rush, barely getting on before it leaves. The driver says he's going back along Granville Street. I get off at my stop and head home. The rain pelts down on my head so strong it hurts. From the street, I can see that there are lights on in the apartment. I see Mama at the window. It's almost eleven o'clock at night.

I knock on the door gingerly. Mama opens it. She is in her housecoat.

"Where have you been?" she asks in an almost normal tone of voice. I feel encouraged. "Mama, I need to talk to you. Where is Max?"

"Max is in bed reading.

"I need to talk to you, too," says Mama, handing me a piece of paper. It was a letter from Tad and they had opened it.

"How dare you open my mail?" My forehead feels sweaty with anger.

"What else can I do when you've been acting so strange! It's for your own good. Max and I want to help you."

I don't approve of this kind of help.

Mama and I sit down in two chairs facing one another. I read the letter.

Dear Slava,

Just a quick note with the latest news. Mortynski has been sentenced. He gave up the deeds to your father's property, and thus got a lighter sentence.

We went through his papers and found Teresa's documents. She isn't really his niece, but seems to have belonged to a Jewish family from Lodz. It is thought that both her parents died in Auschwitz. They left Mortynski a great deal of money to look after her, so he placed her in the convent. Persuaded her to become a nun and thus got rid of her, pocketing most of the money. I couldn't find out anything about your sister Basia, but I will keep looking. In the meantime, here is Teresa's address, in case you don't have it. Perhaps you can help her. You said yourself that she is one of the lost ones. Many Jewish children whose parents didn't come back for them after the war were brought up Catholic without knowing their Jewish roots. Teresa may be one of them.

Love and best wishes
Tadeusz

I try not to show Mama how deeply moved I am by Tad's

letter. But I know that I have to deal with her now, once and for all.

"I am sorry for having done all this without letting you know," I say. I do feel empathy for Mama.

Silence.

"And another thing Mama. I am not going to marry Adam." Mama's face is very serious, but she is not in tears.

"So what do you intend to do with your life, Slava? Become a bum? Adam is a nice steady boy. You won't find another like him."

Mama's lack of faith in me makes me want to rebel even more.

"I have other plans," I respond firmly.

My mother looks at me as if I were out of my mind.

I tell her about Joshua, Montreal, college, and Mrs. Silverman.

"You want to leave here. Live with strangers?"

"You had no qualms about sending me to a boarding school," I challenge.

"I'll have to think about all this, Slava. Now we're all tired. Let's go to bed."

Mama is being evasive.

"Mama, before you go. This thing about Basia. I really tried to find her. I found this girl; her name is Teresa and I thought she was Basia, but it turned out that she wasn't. Something strange has happened to Basia."

"I know," Mama replies. "I've always felt that your father made a deal with Mortynski. Maybe he let him keep Basia so that Mortynski wouldn't tell the Gestapo about us, which he had threatened to do." Mama pauses. "We may never know the truth, Slava. It went with your father to his grave." Mama begins to weep.

"Could this be true?" I go on mercilessly. "Why did we never talk about this?"

Mama shakes her head. She is unable to speak.

I show her Teresa's photograph.

Mama looks at the photograph for a long time. The clock ticks away. Somewhere a fly is buzzing. You can hear our breathing. I can sense Papa's presence in the shadows as I wait for Mama's answer.

"I cannot tell you what you want to know for sure. I don't think this girl is your sister..."

Mama's voice breaks off.

I move closer and try to comfort her.

"I understand your feelings, Mama. But couldn't we help this poor girl? In memory of Basia at least?"

Mama looks up at me with red eyes. "I suppose so," she says slowly. "From what you tell me she needs help. We will try to help her. But you know," she looks at the bedroom door where Max is, "we don't have such great means ourselves. Maybe we can send her a parcel and a letter every so often. Maybe after a time, when she gets older, we could even invite her to come out and visit us." Mama hesitates, then continues. "I'll have to speak to Max about it."

Mama doesn't sound too confident, but she is in control of her emotions now. I kiss her good night and go to my room.

I think of Teresa. Strange how I'm still left not knowing the truth. But somehow, I feel that helping her could perhaps compensate a little for what we couldn't do for Basia when she needed us. I wish Papa were here now. He'd help.

All night I toss and turn, unable to wait till tomorrow. At least, I feel relieved of all the secrets, all but one: Tad. The rest is out in the open. I hope they let me go live in Montreal.

In the morning I wake up from a dreamless sleep, feeling sluggish.

Mama is in the kitchen, chopping vegetables for soup. Max has left for work.

"What would you do if we said, no, you can't leave Vancouver?" Mama says ominously.

"Max doesn't want me here!" I cry. "You know that. I will leave anyway, with or without your permission."

Mama looks surprised. She was used to my being a very obedient daughter until I decided to go to England.

"I suppose if you've made up your mind, there is nothing more I can say." Mama sounds disappointed. I have never measured up to her expectations. I've known that all along.

"Mama," I say gently. "I love you. I don't want to hurt you. But this is about my life. Let me at least try. If it doesn't work I'll come back, I promise."

I put my arms around her. We seem close for the first time in ages. And it feels good.

"I don't want to lose you, too. I've already lost one child. I know Max is not your father, but he wants the best for you. Be reasonable."

I try to understand. So hard. Maybe I don't understand Mama. I don't know what it's like to lose a child. I hope I never will know. Mama has suffered greatly, but I can't sacrifice my right to my own life because of her pain. Besides, no one has that power. Not even Mama. The choices are mine to make.

"I need you to talk to Miriam's mom and tell her it's OK with you."

Mama puts the chopped vegetables into the cauliflower soup. Then, after a long silence, she nods with resignation. I give her Mrs. Silverman's telephone number. I go to my room and write a letter to Joshua, informing him of my decision to return to Montreal.

At dinner Max doesn't speak to me.

Several days go by. A packet of poems and a note arrive from Mur. He promises to send me money as soon as I return the translated poems. The money I'll earn will pay for my ticket to Montreal.

The poems are beautiful and moving. The title of his new collection is *Return to Poland*. It affirms all that I had felt myself when I was there. Just doing them is payment enough.

I start work, and lose myself in it until it's finished. The day I post Mur's poems, two letters arrive. One from Mrs. Silverman, the other from Joshua.

Mrs. Silverman confirms receiving Mama's permission to have me stay at her house. She says that I am welcome.

Joshua writes:

Dearest Liz,

I can't believe our good luck. I really didn't think your
folks would let you come. I am very happy. And Liz,
don't worry about anything. You've always got me. I
know that it's too soon to say this, but some day,
when you can trust me again, we can make more plans
for our future.

All my love
Joshua

© Patti-Gail Bland

Award-winning author Lillian Boraks-Nemetz is a child survivor of the Holocaust. Once in Canada, she attended St. Margaret's School in Victoria, BC, then completed her masters degree in Comparative Literature at the University of British Columbia where she now teaches Creative Writing in the Department of Continuing Studies.

In addition to *The Lenski File*, Lillian has published two previous works of fiction: *The Old Brown Suitcase*, winner of the Sheila A. Egoff BC Book Award and other prizes, and *The Sunflower Diary*, nominated for The Red Maple Reading Award. Her latest collection of poetry is *Ghost Children*.

Boraks-Nemetz has also written a number of essays on post-Holocaust survival, and has translated and co-translated several volumes of poems by Polish émigré poets in Canada.

The author gives frequent talks on racism to elementary and secondary students.

She lives and writes in Vancouver, Canada.

Reference p. 161: The Kielce incident is documented in *The Holocaust*, Martin Gilbert, Fontana Press, London 1987, p. 819